# The Silent Christmas

**A Jayne Sinclair
Genealogical Mystery**

M. J. Lee

## About M. J. Lee

Martin Lee is the author of two different series of historical crime novels; The *Jayne Sinclair Genealogical Mysteries* and the *Inspector Danilov* series set in 1930s Shanghai. *The Silent Child* is the fifth book featuring genealogical investigator, Jayne Sinclair.

## ALSO BY M. J. LEE

*Jayne Sinclair Series*
The Irish Inheritance
The Somme Legacy
The American Candidate
The Vanished Child

*Inspector Danilov Series*
Death in Shanghai
City of Shadows
The Murder Game

*Historical Fiction*
Samuel Pepys and the Stolen Diary
The Fall

"Christmas is a season not only of rejoicing
but of reflection."

Winston Churchill

# Contents

# Chapter One

Monday, December 21, 1914
Neuve Eglise, Belgium

He lay on his back on the hard ground and dreamt of England; picnicking on the grass in front of the bandstand, straw hat tipped over his eyes to shield them from the sun. Next to him, his wife, Norah, poured out another glass of pale ale and placed it next to his hand. On the stand the band played the *Death or Glory March* with the sousaphone slightly off the beat. Somewhere, John and Hetty were running around playing tag with the other children, their high-pitched squeals adding a note of urgency to the music.

A shadow crossed his face and he felt a tap against his foot.

'Time to get up, Tom. We're moving forward.'

In the distance next to the lake, he could hear the shouts of Captain Lawson chivvying the men along. Reluctantly, he sat upright, yawned and said, 'What's his hurry? As long as we get there before nightfall...'

He let the rest of the sentence trail away as so many other sentences had recently, vanishing into the cold, damp air of Flanders in December.

His pal, Bert, shrugged his shoulders. 'You know what it's like in the army. Hurry, hurry. Stop, stop. Hurry again.'

Tom Wright climbed slowly to his feet, wiping the dried mud from his puttees and boots. 'Nowt ever changes, does it?'

Across the clearing, next to the bombed-out farmhouse, Harry Larkin was rushing towards them carrying three tin mugs of milky tea.

'Sorry, lads, it's cold. Half the bloomin' army was lined up.' He handed across the lukewarm mugs. 'Down the hatch, as the actress said to the bishop.'

'No rum?' Bert grumbled.

'Not a drop. QM said it hadn't come up yet. But at least two of the cooks were pissed, so I think they've had their fill already.'

'Bastards,' mumbled Bert, slurping his milky tea through his walrus moustache.

'You went to say goodbye to the French girl, didn't you?'

A broad smile crossed Harry's face. 'I can't tell a lie. Mimi has the sweetest lips in France.' He kissed the ends of his fingers and let them fly away from his face.

Tom shook his head. 'You're going to get caught one day by some big, hairy French husband.'

'Ah, but while the cat's away, the mice will play. And this little mouse likes to play with the French cheese. Talking about cheese, Mimi gave me this.' He pulled out a wedge of soft white Brie from under his jacket. 'Smells a bit but she said it was good to eat.'

He took a bite before handing it to Bert, who sniffed it cautiously before nibbling the end and then immediately drinking his milky tea to wash it down. 'What I wouldn't give for a hunk of Cheshire and a wedge of bread; proper stuff, not this French muck. Can't beat a good chunk of Cheshire cheese.'

Bert was a regular. Been in the army and the Regiment since before the Boer War, joined when he was sixteen. But even though he was only thirty-four, he looked far older. He'd come across with the Cheshires in the early days of the war, fighting though the retreat from the Marne, Mons and the Aisne, even surviving the Battle of Audregnies without a scratch when only six officers and 178 men had come through out of 910 men who had started the attack that morning.

Bert had transferred across to the 6th Battalion when it arrived in France in November to bolster the ranks of reservists such as Tom and Harry. Despite the difference in their seniority, the men had found friendship in the long dreary marches of that long and even drearier autumn.

'Sergeant!'

Bert instantly stood to attention, spilling some of the tea on the front of his overcoat.

'Make sure your platoon is ready to move. I want to relieve the Norfolks by four p.m.'

It was Captain Lawson, who had approached soundlessly as they were drinking their tea.

'Yes, sir,' Bert answered loudly, before turning to his mates and mouthing 'bloody idiot' and rolling his eyes.

He finished the tea in one immense swallow and turned to the men lying on the ground, leaning against the wall of the farm or just standing talking to one another. 'You heard the hofficer, let's be 'avin' you.'

The men began packing up, accompanied by a chorus of grumbles and moans. As they did so, a solitary shell from a German whizz-bang whistled overhead, landing one hundred yards past the farm.

None of the men moved or even ducked; each one carried on preparing to move forward as if nothing had happened.

It was Tom that spoke. 'Looks like they are targeting the farm. I'd get the men moving a little quicker if I were you.'

Bert stared at him and then up at the sky, as if trying to spot another shell in flight through the air. 'Get a move on, you lot. We leave in two minutes.'

This shout was followed by the whine of another shell, this time landing much closer.

Tom picked up his pack and slung it over his shoulder, taking hold of the rope of the ammunition box while Harry took up the other side. They both joined the long line of men trudging wearily towards the front.

As they moved forwards, they passed the mangled remains of an artillery horse and rider ten yards off the path. The man's back was arched and his hand frozen, fingers pointing upwards as if to touch the sun.

Tom averted his eyes, concentrating on placing one foot in front of the other on the slimy path leading forwards. He attempted to return to his memories of that warm day in summer with his wife and children, but much as he tried, they wouldn't come back.

Instead, he stumbled forward, his eyes fixed on the back of the man in front of him. The rain began to fall, in large, heavy drops at first before turning into a steady, inexorable drizzle.

Would he ever see his family again?

## Chapter Two

Friday, December 22, 2017
Central Library, Manchester

'The past is a foreign country. They do things differently there.'

Jayne Sinclair always started her presentations with the same quotation from L. P. Hartley. For her, it perfectly described the problems inherent in family history. Memories of our relatives were distant, intangible, unreliable and often lost.

'Our role as genealogists is to use our research to bring these lost people, the vanished people of our family, back to life.'

Despite it being only three days until Christmas, the audience in Central Library was large for a lunchtime lecture on a dreary, dull Friday. A peculiar English smell hung over the auditorium; the odour of slightly damp raincoats, very damp shoes and drying people. Perhaps it was because the weather was so unpredictable that the audience was so big, she thought to herself as she moved on to the next slide in her PowerPoint presentation.

She had given this particular lecture many times before. It was her standard – 'seven ways you can discover more about your family history' – and was designed as a gentle introduction to genealogy. She illustrated her talk with examples from her own experience: the case of the adopted American billionaire who turned out to have Irish roots; the unfortunate history of the Lassiter family; and one of her more recent cases, the soul-destroying history of Harry Britton, one of the migrant children sent to Australia after World War Two.

She finished her half-hour presentation and, as she always did, opened the floor to questions. After the usual embarrassed silence in the audience and the requisite number of coughs, a woman in the front row stood up.

'What about DNA? Do you think the latest advances will change how we investigate our families?'

'Thank you for a great question. The recent advances in DNA have already changed the way genealogists work. In one of my recent cases, I investigated the family origins of a young celebrity who discovered that she had African ancestry in her DNA.'

The woman in the front row nudged her neighbour. 'That was the Emily Marlowe case, wasn't it?'

'Through family history research, we managed to show where the African ancestor originated, revealing a whole new side to Emily's family she never knew existed.'

Another hand went up. 'Which websites would you recommend for family history research?'

This was quite a common question. 'The two big ones are Ancestry and Findmypast. Both have their strengths and weaknesses, but both are great starting points in the journey to discover your family. Lost Cousins is another great site, particularly if you want to extend your family connections or break down walls.'

'Walls?' the woman in the front row asked.

'Walls are when there is a link missing to a past relative. Either we haven't found the document with the ancestor's name yet or the document doesn't exist.

To go back further in the past, we need to break down the wall.'

Another hand went up, from a man sitting next to a young boy. 'Do you ever use objects to help you research a family?'

'All the time. The object obviously does not directly link us to family history but it gives us a new opening, a new window if you like, into that ancestor's life. For example, one client had a medallion with a purple, white and green ribbon. A little research helped me discover that the medallion was given to members of the Women's Social and Political Union, also known as the Suffragettes.'

The questions continued for the next ten minutes. When the clock at the back of the hall reached 1.55 p.m., Jayne thanked the audience and brought the presentation to an end. After a smattering of applause, people began to leave the auditorium, all except the man and the young boy, who remained seated.

Jayne packed her bags and her computer and began to leave. As she did so, they both stepped into the aisle, blocking her way.

'Thank you for the presentation, Mrs Sinclair, it was very interesting.'

'I'm glad you enjoyed it, Mr...?'

He handed across a bright blue card with what looked like a pink lightning flash on it. 'The name's Wright. David Wright, I'm an electrician. And this is my son, Martin.'

Jayne reached forward and ruffled the boy's hair. 'I'm happy that somebody so young is interested in family history.'

'We have a reason. You see...' David Wright paused mid-sentence almost as if he were embarrassed.

Jayne waited for him to continue. When she was a detective in the police, she found silence was always the most useful weapon in any interview. Rather than rush in and speak, she would let the witness fill the vacuum. Often what they said then was more important than any question they answered.

'We found these things carefully wrapped up in an old chest in our attic and we wondered if you could help us.'

The boy smiled and lifted up a Tesco carrier bag.

'You've been shopping?' asked Jayne.

'Show her, Martin,' the father said gently.

The boy reached into the bag and pulled out a piece of wrinkled and cracked leather, shaped like one of those wooden fruit bowls that were popular throughout the 1970s and could now be bought from IKEA.

'What is it?' Jayne asked, bending down to look at the object more closely.

David Wright smiled. 'That's what we want you to find out, Mrs Sinclair.'

## Chapter Three

Tuesday, December 22, 1914
Wulverghem, Belgium

The brazier burnt with a warm, red glow, the men huddled over it, their bodies attempting to absorb every last ray of heat. All the time, they stamped their army boots in the sludge of the trench, desperately trying to retain a semblance of life in their cold feet.

The trench itself was a ragged affair; a wall of sandbags built up in front of a shallow ditch to form a parapet, into which had been inserted observation posts. Every twenty yards or so, a wooden roof betrayed the presence of a shallow dugout lined with straw. In front of the line, barbed wire stretched along the ground like a creeping vine, wild in its confusion.

A former turnip field sloped gently upwards to the German lines two hundred yards away. The Germans, from their elevated vantage point, could see most of what was happening in the British trenches, particularly when the snipers were active. All the soldiers of Bert's platoon quickly became adept at keeping their heads down below the parapet.

They had been lucky that evening. A warm stew of bully beef had been delivered in billycans to the front line, followed by cocoa and the obligatory tot of rum.

'Must be Christmas,' said Bert, 'even the food is warm.'

Tom grunted and swallowed the last of the hot chocolate. The crack of a rifle bullet was followed by a soft thud as it struck the revetment of the trench twenty yards away.

'Keep your 'eads down,' shouted Bert over his shoulder.

'Fritz is busy tonight,' said Harry.

As if to confirm his words, another bullet whined over their heads.

'You know, right now, me and the wife would normally be going to Victoria market to find us a bird. A goose is what I'd choose, if it weren't too expensive, mind. Mister Brocklehurst would always let us leave early in the days before Christmas, five o'clock instead of the usual six thirty. He was good like that.'

'Where did you work?'asked Bert

'At Bankwood Mill. I was a cotton piecer. Not a bad job and we got every Sunday off. Mister Brocklehurst was a Methodist, couldn't abide people working on Sundays. Had to go to church, though, even if you were Catholic. Black mark against your name if you weren't seen in a church. What about you, Harry?'

'Mum was a Catholic but Dad worshipped down the local pub.' He stared into the embers of the fire and laughed. 'Liked to worship there every night, he did.'

'I meant what work did you do in civvy street?'

'Not a lot. This and that.'

'This and that, what?'

'One job I had was delivering milk. But I didn't last long. I could never remember who got what, when, where or how much. That was, of course, when I could remember to get up.'

'Yeah, a milkman that can't get up in the morning. Could be a problem,' said Bert.

'That wasn't why I got sacked. Nah, they were okay about that. It was the hoss that did me in.'

'The hoss?' asked Tom.

Harry stretched his fingers in their cut-off mittens in front of the brazier. His words came out like little puffs of smoke in the cold night air.

'The nag didn't like me. I used to tell it to go one way, it went the other. I tried to feed it, it refused to eat. I think it complained to the boss one day and I was sacked.'

'The hoss complained to the boss?'

'I'm sure it did. The boss came up to me one day. As cool as Lillie Langtry he says, "The hoss and you aren't getting on. Now, I can get milkmen any day of the week but I can't get a hoss like that." So I was out on my arse. As I was taking off my apron and walking to the office to pick up my wages, I heard the hoss give a loud whinny. It was like the bastard were saying, "Piss off and don't come back." I got my revenge, though, didn't I?'

'What do you mean?'

At this, Harry leant in closer as if telling a secret. 'Nipped back later that night, didn't I? Put some ball bearings in his feed. I pity the poor bugger sitting behind the hoss next morning.'

With a self-satisfied look on his face, Harry sat back and smiled. 'I was glad anyway when they gave me the sack. Being a milkman wasn't what I wanted to do for the rest of my life.'

'I suppose you had an 'igher callin'?' said Bert, nudging Tom's elbow.

'Gonna be a footballer when this lot's over.'

'Footballer?'

'Aye, had a trial with Stockport County, I did. Said I was a good little winger.'

'So how'd you end up in the army?'

21

'I was a reservist so called up, wasn't I? Said they'd keep my place when I returned after Christmas, though.'

Tom looked around him. 'It's nearly Christmas and we're still here.'

'True. But it'll be over soon and I can go back and play. The league is still going.'

'I wouldn't be so certain, Harry. I heard his little lot is going on for at least another three months,' said Tom.

A star shell rocketed up into the sky and drifted down over no-man's-land, illuminating the gap between the two trenches in a bright white light.

Tom leant closer to the fire, trying to find more heat from the dying embers. 'Fritz is active tonight. What about you?'

Bert sat up straighter. 'Regular, me. Joined in 1896. Nineteen years next March I'll have, plus two good conduct medals. Might make Colour Sergeant with a bit of luck, if I keep my nose clean.'

Another bullet whined over their heads.

'And if you can avoid one of those.'

'You won't find me taking any risks. Eighteen years in the army has taught me to look after myself — no bloody heroics and never, ever volunteer.'

Tom nodded. 'Good advice, but why'd you join in the first place?'

Bert shrugged his shoulders. 'There was an army recruiting office and they were looking for volunteers. And besides, it was either going down the pit or joining up. Which would you choose?'

Nobody answered, all three of them just staring into the embers of the brazier, now with a white ash frosting the burning wood.

'Sergeant.' It was Captain Lawson, who had crept up on them silently again through the slime. 'Fritz is a bit friendly this evening. Make sure the sentries stay alert. Two hours on, four off.'

'Yes, sir.'

'Keep the bombs handy, but don't lob any into no-man's-land without my express orders. Understood?'

'Yes, sir.'

'Carry on, Sergeant.'

Captain Lawson moved on past them, sliding down the rest of the trench towards C Company.

Bert turned back towards them and mouthed 'bloody idiot'.

'He's not a bad sort. I've known worse,' said Harry.

'He's young and he's stupid. Barely out of school trousers.'

'Writes a diary and poetry, so I've heard.'

'Poetry?' exploded Bert.

'Heard it from his batman. Sits there staring into mid-air with a book in front of him and a stupid look on his face. Occasionally, he leans forward and writes a few words.'

'Are you sure it's poetry?' asked Harry.

'That's what his batman said. Mind you, John Wainwright – that's the batman's name – was never great at reading. Went to school with him, I did.'

'Poetry,' muttered Bert, shaking his head. 'Just what we bloody need. A soldier who writes poetry. What use is that to anybody?'

Seconds later a bullet crashed into the wood above their heads. Instinctively, they ducked as a few splinters flew through the air.

'That's what we need, a good sniper. Not a bloody poet.'

'Shh...' Tom stopped him from talking, '...listen.'

'Hello, Tommy.'

The voice was far away, coming from the German trenches.

'Waiter, bring me cream cakes,' shouted Harry, cupping his hand near his mouth and stretching up towards the top of the parapet.

'Very funny, Tommy. Not all waiters in Germany, I was a mechanic in Manchester.'

'Well, I never...' said Bert.

'I thought I recognised the Manchester accent,' said Harry.

'What are you doing over there?' shouted Tom over the parapet.

There was a long pause. 'Fighting, just like you. Merry Christmas, Tommy.'

'Merry Christmas, Fritz.'

Then it all went quiet. Above them, a half-moon peered from behind the clouds and a harmonica in the next platoon began playing *Danny Boy*.

'Manchester...' said Harry. 'I wonder if he supports United or City?'

## Chapter Four

Friday, December 22, 2017
Central Library, Manchester

Jayne examined the leather object closely. It was about nine inches in diameter and concave in shape, the leather stiff and wrinkled with age like the skin of an old man. It seemed to be divided into sections and was hollow on the inside. A few stitches had come undone from one of the sections and, peering inside the dark interior, a decayed piece of what looked like string was resting across a rubber tube. 'I haven't a clue what it could be and I'm not an antiques dealer, Mr Wright,' she said, handing it back.

'I know, but that's why we came to see you. My other son Chris found it when we were clearing out the attic in Mum's house. She died a week ago...'

'I'm sorry for your loss.' Jayne found herself mumbling the words. Why was she always embarrassed when somebody mentioned death in her presence?

'Mum had a good life, a long life. By the end, I think she wanted to go to meet my father, his granddad.' He patted the boy on his head. 'We think this belonged to him. It was wrapped up in a chest in the attic.'

'I think you should take it to a good antiques dealer. I'm sure he'll be able to tell you what it is.' Jayne tried to edge past him, but he stood his ground.

'There's something else we found with it that I want you to see.'

From the interior of the Tesco bag the man produced a round silver object, the colour on the surface slightly faded and tarnished with age, as if somebody had been rubbing their thumb over it. The number 35 was embossed in the middle.

'It looks like a coin.'

'Or a button,' piped up the young boy.

Jayne pursed her lips. 'You could be right, Martin.'

'That's what Chris thought too. We found one final thing in the chest.'

He reached into the bag and brought out a piece of paper shaped like a luggage tag with two thin pieces of string running from a reinforced hole at the top. One side of the tag was printed with a green design and strange angular lettering. On the other side, a name and address were written in an ink that had browned with age:

*Tom Wright 12725*
*22, Elgin Street,*
*Stalybridge*

Beside the address in a different hand, and larger, were the numbers 3-2. These numbers had not faded so much with time.

David reached over and tapped the tag. 'This was tied to to the leather object. Tom Wright. That was my grandfather's name. He died when I was a young boy in 1976. I don't remember much about him. He didn't speak a lot, a quiet man, worked all his life as a postman in Stalybridge until he retired. After that, he worked on his allotment. I always remember him smoking his pipe, though. Can still remember the smell today. It's funny how things like that stay with you – smells, I mean.'

Jayne liked this man and his son, but it was the week before Christmas, she hadn't bought any presents yet for Robert, her dad, or Vera, his new wife. She hadn't even ordered the turkey and they were coming to her house for Christmas dinner. Her father had accepted the invitation even though he knew she wasn't the best cook in the world. At least the wine would be good. She had saved a couple of bottles of Chateau Lynch-Bages as a special treat.

'...so you see, that's why it's important to us.'

She realised the man had been speaking all the time she had been thinking about making Christmas dinner. 'Sorry, I missed that.'

The man swallowed and began again. 'My other son, Chris. He's in hospital at the moment. In Christie's.'

The name of Manchester's hospital for treating cancer sent alarm bells ringing in Jayne's head. 'I hope he's not too poorly.'

'Juvenile leukaemia.'

'I'm sorry.'

'He was diagnosed last month and they took him in three days ago. He'll be in over Christmas, starts chemo after the holiday. We're off to see him this afternoon.'

'I'm very sorry, Mr Wright. How old is he?'

The man's eyes went down to the floor. 'Fourteen. He's my eldest.'

The young boy spoke. 'You see, we promised Chris... I promised Chris that we would find out all about the button and the label and the leather thing we found in our grandfather's trunk. It was going to be my Christmas present to him.'

'But we've looked everywhere on the internet and can't find anything about them. And we haven't even got a clue what this is.' He held up the leather object. 'We were in town doing some late Christmas shopping and saw you were giving a talk and came along. Can you help us, Mrs Sinclair?'

Jayne sighed and shook her head. 'I'm sorry, Mr Wright. An antique dealer could do far better than me. At least he would know what this is.'

'But it's the label that's important. It's got my grandfather's name on it. You could find out what it is by researching him, couldn't you?'

Jayne thought for a moment. She could perhaps perform a quick search on the man's grandfather, at least find out his background – it wouldn't take long. But it was Christmas and she had so much to do...

Her phone rang.

'Excuse me.' She delved into her handbag. Where was the bloody thing? The sound of ringing was becoming louder and more persistent. Where was it?

The young boy tapped her on the arm and pointed to her laptop bag. The ringing was coming from inside there. She checked the name on the screen. It was Vera, her stepmother.

'Hi, Vera—'

'It's Robert, he collapsed. They've rushed him to hospital.'

# Chapter Five

Friday, December 22, 2017
Macclesfield General Hospital, Cheshire

'We can't go in yet. The doctor's examining him.'
Vera blocked Jayne from going through the door into
the ward.

'What happened? Is he okay? What's wrong with
him?'

On hearing the news, Jayne had rushed out of
Central Library and ran to her car, which was parked
nearby. It had taken her fifty minutes to drive to Macclesfield Hospital, where her father had been taken.
She was sure she had accelerated past at least two
speed cameras in the drive down the A523, but she
didn't care. All that mattered was Robert. Was he still
alive? She wanted to talk to him one more time. To
tell him how much she loved him.

Vera took her by the arm. 'He's not been feeling
well for the last few days. Said it was difficult to
breathe. I thought he had a spot of winter flu, nothing to worry about. Then this morning, we'd had our
breakfast at the home and were walking down the
corridor to the TV room to do the crossword – you
know how much Robert loves to do his crosswords –
when he just collapsed. I thought he'd had a heart
attack. Luckily Matron was there and she called the
ambulance. We went straight to A&E and they admit-

ted him within an hour. We were lucky there was a bed free.'

All the while, Vera had been speaking in a quiet, calm voice, her hand holding Jayne's arm.

Jayne took three deep breaths, trying to quieten her beating heart. 'He's going to be okay, isn't he?'

Vera didn't answer, just patted her hand.

A doctor and a nurse came out of the room and walked over to them. 'Mrs Cartwright?'

Vera put her hand up. 'I'm Mrs Cartwright and this is Robert's daughter, Jayne.'

The doctor nodded towards Jayne but spoke to Vera. 'Robert has a bad case of double pneumonia. We've given him antibiotics and he's on a saline drip. At the moment, we're just using oxygen through a mask, but if his condition worsens we'll have to move him to ICU and put him on a ventilator.'

'He's going to be okay, isn't he, Doctor?

The doctor, a young Asian man, looked down at the ground. 'He's comfortable for the moment, but such an attack puts an immense strain on the heart of a man his age. We'll keep monitoring him constantly. It's just a question of time now.'

'Can we go in and see him?'

The doctor looked at the nurse, who nodded. 'For a few minutes. He's sleeping and the best thing is for him to rest and let the antibiotics work. If you'll excuse me, I must continue with my rounds, there are other patients to see.'

The nurse gestured with her hand. 'Come with me.'

She opened the door and they stepped in. The room was a four-bed ward, the three other beds occupied by older people who were either sleeping or reading. One bed had the blinds drawn around it. This was Robert's bed.

The nurse pulled one side back and allowed them to step forward.

Jayne's father was lying in bed, a tube attached to the back of his hand from a saline drip above his head. A clear plastic oxygen mask covered his nose and mouth. Two other machines beeped quietly and slowly, monitoring his life signs.

Lying there unmoving, he looked so vulnerable, so fragile to Jayne. So different from the strong, intelligent man she knew as her father. She felt Vera touch her arm and she looked at her stepmother's face, the eyes red-rimmed, just about holding back her tears.

She looked back at Robert and, without bidding, a memory sprang into her mind.

They both stood outside the doors of Manchester Museum. She must have been 14 or 15, for most of that week had been spent arguing with her mother. It was the typical type of fight that teenagers get into with their parents. Her skirts were either too short or too long. Her hair then was styled in the curls of Kylie Minogue, which her mother said made her look like a poodle on heat. The final bone of contention was her boyfriend at that time, Gerry. A lovely lad who looked like Jason Donovan and was an apprentice plumber. It was one Saturday morning when it all kicked off.

'I'm having no daughter of mine having a relationship with a man who spends most of his time up to his elbows in shit.'

'Mum, he spends most of his time making tea and laying bathroom tiles.'

'He's too old for you.'

'He's only twenty-one.'

'You told me he was eighteen?'

Jayne had forgotten the little white lie she had first told her mother about Gerry.

'He's too old. I'm not having it, understand, little lady?'

'Oh, I can see you're not having it, that's why you're so irritable all the time.'

Her mother stared at her for a moment before the arm came round in a wide arc and struck Jayne on her face. The blow didn't hurt but the shock did. How dare her mother strike her? She went to lift her own hand when Robert caught it and ushered her out of the house before she did any real damage.

They ended up at Manchester Museum.

'Look, lass, your mother means well. She cares for you.'

'Hitting your daughter across the face is a funny way of showing it.'

'Sometimes, people can't say the words...'

'By people, you mean my mother?'

'She loves you, Jayne.'

'How do you put up with her, Robert?'

As her stepfather, she had always called him by his Christian name. Her biological father had walked out on them when she was only three months old. Robert had married her mother three years later and, for Jayne, he was the only father she had ever known.

'I love your mother. Always have done, always will do.'

'Despite her temper?'

'Because of her temper.'

'You're a strange man, Robert.'

'And I love you too, always remember that, lass.'

They had gone into the museum and spent hours looking at the mummies in their cases. She realised later it was Robert's understated way of telling her that all the rows would pass. Nothing lasts for ever. These 3000-year-old mummies had once lived and laughed and loved and argued and now they were nothing but shrivelled bodies in a museum.

He was a subtle man was Robert.

God, she loved him.

She felt the nurse's hand on her elbow. 'It's time to leave now.'

Jayne nodded and, taking one last look at her father lying motionless in his bed, helped Vera leave the room.

# Chapter Six

Wednesday, 23 December, 1914
Wulverghem, Belgium

Overnight the temperature had dropped. Frost rimed the mud of no-man's-land, like whitecaps on a troubled sea. The stench of dead bodies from the German attack five days ago hhad dissipated, but the bodies still remained, intermingled with the Tommies who had died with them. The corpse of one soldier was still draped over the wire where he had fallen.

'It's not right, leaving him out there on the wire.'

It was Harry speaking. He now wore a woollen fleece overcoat, 'liberated' from a sergeant in the Manchesters, who had made the mistake of leaving it hanging on a hook when he went to the latrine.

'I mean, would you like to be left out there, if you ever copped it?'

Bert didn't answer. He was busy darning a hole in his sock. His pasty feet with their large horny nails were out of his boots and being aired in front of the fire.

'Got to look after your feet, them's a man's best friend, they is,' he said, squinting down at the heel of the sock.

'I thought that was dogs.'

'It's feet. Keep your feet looked after and they'll look after you.' He stopped darning for a moment and rubbed the end of his big toe, poking his finger carefully between each of his other toes, removing any dirt that had collected there. Then he went back to his darning, ensuring that the repair to the heel was perfect.

'Fritz is quiet this morning. The ten o'clock hate hasn't started yet.'

Tom stared at his Borget, a prized possession given to him by Mr Brocklehurst the day he was called up as a reservist and left for the front. 'There ye are, lad. With this you'll always know the time. It's an officer's watch, no tat for one of my workers. Luminous dial so ye can see in't dark. And don't worry, lad, your job will still be here waiting for you when you come back at Christmas. Papers say it'll all be over by then. We'll have chased the Kaiser back down his hole.'

Now it was nearly Christmas and the war still wasn't over.

'Perhaps the Fritz artillery have gone home for the holidays,' said Harry.

As if on cue, the shells of the Whistling Willies flew over their heads, landing somewhere in the communication lines at the rear.

'No Coal Boxes or Flying Pigs today,' said Bert, listening to the sounds of the explosions behind them.

'At least it's not us. Some other poor bastards are copping it.'

'As long as it's not the cooks.' Bert slipped the sock back over his foot, checking his handiwork. 'An army marches on its stomach. Some general said that.'

'I thought it marched on its feet?' asked Harry, his forehead creasing into a frown.

A sergeant bustled towards them down the trench, keeping his head well below the parapet as the shells whistled over.

'Mail's come,' said Harry.

The sergeant was a lifer from HQ Company who had managed to luck into a cushy number as the clerk to the quartermaster. His only dangerous job was delivering the mail to the men when it arrived, which was usually long after it had been sent.

This time he carried a large hessian sack and dropped it at their feet, rummaging inside. 'You're in luck, lads, special delivery courtesy of Princess Mary.' He brought out three brass tins, each one stamped with the head of a young woman and the letters 'MM' on either side. 'You don't smoke, do you, Harry?'

'Knackers the football, don't it?'

'This one's for you, then.' He passed over one of the brass tins. 'You two take pot luck.'

Bert took the tin on the left while Tom took the one on the right.

'Wright, you got a parcel. Only posted on the fourteenth, they must have run with it from Dover. Special courier, like.' The sergeant laughed at his own joke. 'Harry, you got a box.' He took it out of his sack and stared at the postmark. 'Sent last October.' He smelt the box. 'Hope they haven't put food in. Will be as ripe as a Salford arse if they have.'

He passed the box across to Harry, who shook it to hear the contents rattle inside. 'Must be from Doris.'

'Who's Doris?'

'The wife.'

'Didn't know you were married?'

Harry winked. 'I'm not, till I go back to Blighty.'

The sergeant stood up to leave, but his sleeve was caught by Bert. 'Anything for me?'

The man shook his head. 'Maybe next time.' He then moved down the trench to the next position.

Tom ripped open his parcel quickly. Inside was a long grey scarf, hand-knitted by his wife. 'Well done,

Norah, dear. You got my letter.' As he wound the scarf around his neck and under his jacket, a letter flopped out to land in the slime at the bottom of the trench. He snatched it up, wiped the smears of mud from the envelope and placed it in his top pocket. 'I'll save this for later.'

The other two looked crestfallen. They enjoyed listening to Tom's letters from his wife. But both recognised he had to read it himself first. A man was allowed some privacy even here.

Bert opened his brass tin. Inside was a packet of cigarettes, a smaller pouch of tobacco, a studio picture of Princess Mary staring off into the distance and a Christmas card from King George and Queen Mary.

'I only saw the bugger last week and now I'm on his Christmas card list.'

On December 9, the first battalion of the Cheshires had been paraded for the King on a tour of the front lines. Bert had been transferred across to make up the numbers. He had spent two whole days on spit and polish, making sure he looked spotless for the royal visit.

'You only saw him for a second, Bert. Didn't know you were chums now.'

As a regular, Bert was one of the soldiers chosen to be part of the honour guard for the King. The man had shuffled in front of him, guided by the colonel, even stopping to chat for a second.

'Keep up the good work,' King George had said.

'I will, sir,' replied Bert.

The answer received a stare from the colonel. He wasn't supposed to say anything. The King appeared not to notice and walked on.

Harry had opened his tin now. 'I've got one too, so you're not so special, Bert Simpkins.' He opened the card and read out loud, 'With our best wishes for Christmas 1914. May God protect you and bring you home safe.'

Silence from all three of them for a few seconds.

Around them the war carried on, shells falling a few miles away. Men squeezed past them on their way to another part of the line, the rest of their platoon sleeping or huddling on the straw in the wet dugouts carved into the sides of the trench.

Harry broke the silence. 'And I've got this too.' He opened a tiny paper folder. Inside were envelopes, writing paper and a bullet. 'Why are they sending me a bullet, for God's sake? We got plenty of those.'

Tom snatched it out of his hand. He pulled off the metal top and reversed it to reveal a pencil, which he then slotted into the case of the bullet. 'Now you've got no excuse not to write home to the wife.'

'What's in yours, Tom?'

He opened his tin. Inside were tobacco and cigarettes too and, in a separate pouch, a pipe. He stuck it between his teeth and struck a pose. 'See, makes me look clever, like Sherlock Holmes.'

Harry rattled his box again. 'Wonder what it is? Food, I hope. I'd love a tin of spam or, even better, a link of pork sausages from Frost the butchers. Does a wonderful sausage, does Mr Frost. Won a prize for his sausages, he did.'

'Open the bloody thing and find out,' said Bert grumpily.

Harry ripped open the cover, peered inside and then ripped through some old, yellowed newspapers covering his Christmas gift. He looked inside and reached to pull out a slightly deflated football.

'I've always wanted a football,' said Bert.

Harry peered into the box and then back at the football. 'What was the daft woman thinking? That I

can practise my dribbling while I wait to get killed?'
He threw the ball down the line of the trench, where
it bounced twice and then vanished into a dugout.

'Perhaps there's a letter inside,' said Tom.

At the bottom of the box, Harry found a postcard.

'Hello, love,' he read out loud. 'The *Daily Mirror* is
running a competition to send footballs to our men in
the trenches so I put your name forward. I wrapped it
up in the sports pages of the Manchester Evening
News so as you can see how well City are doing. Got
to go now. Love, Doris.'

'Is that it?' asked Bert.

Harry turned the postcard over. The other side
was blank. 'Doris was never one for words. Much pre-
ferred doing things, if you get my drift. Very affec-
tionate, she is.'

Captain Lawson hurried along the trench. 'Your
platoon's turn for the duty roster, Sergeant. Get your
men together.'

'Yes, sir. Private Wright, you take the first two
hours on post three, and Private Larkin, you can relieve him at noon.'

'Good, carry on.' Lawson continued splashing
down the trench.

'Yes, sir, no, sir, three bags full, sir.' Harry mim-
icked Bert's country voice. 'Can I scratch your arse for
you, sir? Please, sir.'

Bert looked at both of them. It was the look of
their platoon leader, not their friend. 'What are you
waiting for?'

Tom stood up slowly and reluctantly, taking hold
of his rifle.

'And watch out for that sniper. He's already taken
out Rowell in C Company.'

'Yes, sir. Three bags full, sir.'

Tom sloped off to take his place behind the periscope at post three, hoping Fritz would be quiet this Christmas, and feeling the letter from Norah heavy against his chest

# Chapter Seven

Friday, December 22, 2017
Didsbury, Manchester

Jayne opened the door to her home and Mr Smith instantly ran to greet her, rubbing his body and tail against her leg even before she had properly crossed the threshold. Dropping her bags at her feet, she reached down to stroke him. More surprisingly, he then let her pick him up without so much as the suggestion of a struggle. It was as if he understood she needed some love at that moment.

Vera was still at the hospital. It had taken her a long time to persuade Jayne to leave.

'Listen, the doctor said that Robert needs sleep. I'll stay with him while you go home. Both of us don't need to spend the night here.'

'But—' Jayne tried to speak.

'But nothing, Jayne, it would be silly for both of us to sit here all night. I'll call you if anything happens.'

Jayne tried again. 'Let me sit with him then, you go.'

'Go home? You forget, myself and your dad live in a home. It's not so different from here. I'll be okay. Got my knitting, my crossword and my book.' She held up Stephen King's latest offering. 'I'll be comfortable here, don't you worry. And I was a nurse, remember.'

Jayne couldn't argue with the logic. She tried nonetheless. 'But...'

'I need to be here, Jayne.'

Vera softly emphasised the word 'need' and Jayne understood straight away without saying any more. They had been married less than a year. Vera needed to be with her new husband, and Jayne, as the daughter, needed to understand that.

'Okay, but I'll come back tomorrow morning, so you can have a rest.'

'Let me call you first before you drive all the way out from Manchester. Perhaps you can do the evening shift tomorrow?'

Jayne had driven home and now walked into the cold, dark kitchen, carrying Mr Smith in her arms. She nuzzled the soft fur of his stomach with her nose and he immediately twisted out of her arms, ran to his empty bowl and began to mew.

Obviously, she had taken intimacy a step too far. With cats, you always had to recognise the boundaries.

'I know, I know, you're hungry.'

She switched on her computer to check her mail. The cat, meanwhile, continued to whine with all the insistence of a squeaking door. How dare she not attend to his needs immediately? Messages could wait.

She opened the fridge door. None of his usual gourmet cat food was left; no chicken liver and asparagus, no lamb and carrots, no beef supreme. She brought out and opened a bag of dry cat food. 'I'm afraid this is it, Mr Smith. The Sinclair restaurant has run out of your usual delights.' She filled his bowl to the brim and topped up his water from the sink.

Mr Smith approached the bowl cautiously, sniffing constantly before settling down to gnaw at the dry food without a miaow of complaint.

'You must be hungry,' said Jayne out loud.

She went back to the door and picked up her bags, placing them on the desk next to the computer. She thought about having a glass of wine to relax, then decided against it. What happened if Vera called her in the middle of the night and she had to drive back to the hospital? A shiver shuddered down her spine at the thought. 'Please, no phone calls tonight,' she said out loud again.

Nobody answered back. The cat stopped crunching his dry food, looked back towards her for a second and then returned to his evening meal.

Jayne had split up with her husband Paul over a year ago now. There had been a few hiccups over the summer when he met somebody else and wanted a divorce, but it had all been settled amicably, like two grown-ups, and they had agreed to go for the less painful option of a legal separation. It left the issue of their one joint asset – the house – up in the air, but Jayne could live with the uncertainty at the moment. After all, in the greater scheme of things, what did it matter where she lived as long as she and Mr Smith had a roof over their heads somewhere?

She checked her emails. The first was from an old friend in the police force, wishing her a Merry Christmas. She had left Greater Manchester Police five years ago but still remained in touch with her colleagues. She had spent nearly half her life working there, and had loved every second of it until one incident destroyed everything; the death of her partner, DS Dave Gilmour. After that, she couldn't face the work any more. Too much guilt, too much sorrow. It was all too much.

The second and third emails were bills for the gas and electric. The vampires still wanted to be paid even though it was Christmas.

The fourth was from David Wright.

*Dear Mrs Sinclair,*

*Remember me? We met this afternoon at your talk. I found your email address from the website. I know you said you didn't have the time and it was nearly Christmas, but it would mean so much to both my sons if we could find out about my granddad. And at Christmas, there's nothing more important than family.*

*Thank you for your time, even if the answer is still no. Merry Christmas.*

*Best regards, David Wright*

*PS. I hope your father is getting better.*

Jayne started to type her reply: *I'm sorry, Mr Wright, but I regret to...*

Then she stopped, reading the last words of his email again. I hope your father is getting better.

Her mind flashed back to that image of Robert lying in the hospital bed, tubes running out of his body attached to machines and drips, and his face covered in an oxygen mask. His eyes closed, his forehead creased and his grey hair splayed carelessly across the pillow.

At Christmas.

He was in hospital at Christmas.

And then she thought of the young boy, David Wright's eldest son, also stuck in a hospital at Christmas. Ill, lonely, missing his family, hoping his sickness would end soon so he could run out to play, or simply open his presents on Christmas morning with his brother, eating the chocolate and the sweet tangerines from the stocking.

She checked the card in her pocket and rang the mobile number. It was answered after two rings.

'Hello, is that David Wright?' she asked.

'It is, but I'm afraid if you're looking for an electrician, we've closed till after Christmas. I can recommend somebody else who is open, though, if you'd like.'

'It's Jayne Sinclair, Mr Wright. I've decided to aid you in your search if you would still like my help. I can't do it full time, though. I have to go and see my father. He was taken into hospital this afternoon.'

'I'm terribly sorry, Mrs Sinclair, I overheard your phone call... I hope he's okay.'

'He's under sedation at the moment. We're just hoping for the best.'

'I'll pray for him.'

'Thank you. Now, to get started, can you email me everything you know about your family. I can do quite a bit on the computer tonight and, if we could meet tomorrow, I can pick up the objects and the luggage tag. I know somebody who may be able to tell me what they are.'

'I could bring it to you?'

'No worries, I'll pick it up on my way to see Herbert – that's the man who can help us. Let's say nine tomorrow at your place?' Jayne quickly worked out that she could visit Herbert in Cheetham Hill before going to see her father at the hospital. 'Is the address the same as on your business card?'

'It is.' He repeated the address and postcode, just to be sure. She knew the area well and it wasn't far from Cheetham Hill, near Heaton Park. 'I'll see you tomorrow, Mr Wright.'

'Call me David, please. And thank you for doing this, Mrs Sinclair. You don't know what it means to both my sons.'

'It's Christmas, David, it's supposed to be about families coming together. Unfortunately, through circumstances, ours are going to be apart.'

# Chapter Eight

Wednesday, December 23, 1914
Wulverghem, Belgium

Tom had just started his third watch of the day. The evening sky was bright with arcing trails of Very lights; a brilliant white from the English side and a pale yellow from the German. Combined with the light of the moon peering through the clouds, they illuminated no-man's-land, the phosphorescence glinting off the strands of barbed wire. To the left, the body of the dead German was still hanging off the wire, its hand reaching forward as if trying to pick something up from the earth.

Tom peered through the periscope and occasionally popped his head over the top of the trench to take in the whole scene. A year ago on this night he would have been preparing the goose with his wife; pulling out the giblets, stuffing the inside with potatoes and Bramley apples, making the gravy from the offal and the fat left behind in the roasting pan. How he loved roast goose, the skin crispy with fat just bubbling beneath the surface of the bird. He was always given the leg. A Christmas treat, which he attacked, ripping the meat from the carcass and covering his face in grease so he could taste the Christmas goose for days afterwards on his moustache.

His children would be sleeping now. John in his own bed and the girls, Alice and Hetty, sharing with the other. He often stood in the doorway, watching them sleep in the light of the oil lamp, serenity and peace resting on their faces as they dreamt of the future.

What did it hold?

When the war ended - it must come to an end soon - he would go home and build a better world for his children. It wouldn't be long now, neither side could go on like this much longer. The Kaiser and the King would one day sit down and talk together and finish it. Weren't they cousins, after all?

Then they could all go home back to their lives, he to his job at the mill, but not for long. He had his eye on opening a mechanic's shop. He was good with his hands and loved tinkering with motors. Cars were the future, he was sure of it, despite what those men in the cavalry said.

Bert could go back to his spit and polish in some barracks out in India or Ireland, while Harry could do whatever he got up to in Manchester. Something involving thieving and women, no doubt, and not necessarily in that order.

But Tom was going to be different, making a life for himself and his family. It had gone on too long, this war — nearly four months already. It was time to go home.

He popped his head over the top of the parapet. All was quiet in no-man's-land, no patrols from Fritz tonight.

He checked his watch. Still another hour before he was relieved and could get his head down to sleep. Lord, he was tired. Of the war, of being away from the kids. Of being hungry and cold and wet. He was tired of being tired.

On his left, another Very light shot up from the English line, hung at the top of its arc for a second then slowly floated back to earth, illuminating the gap between the lines with its bright light.

He took out Norah's letter from this morning and read it again before the Very light fell to earth and darkness returned. It was dated December 14; she must have written it the night before it was posted.

*Dear Tom,*

*Well, it's nearly Christmas again. This time last year I had just taken out the money from the Christmas Club and I remember coming back from Mr Hargreaves' shop with my purse heavier than a pig's snout.*

*This year, I haven't saved so much, what with you being away and prices in the shops being what they are. The children are looking forward to the holiday, Hetty because she won't have to go to school rather than anything else. John is now a handful, always wanting to play with his soldiers. Alice is a beautiful child, so quiet as she sits in her chair watching the world around her. They'll miss you at Christmas and so will I. But I'll make sure they go to confession and to mass on Christmas Eve. I'm having no heathens in my house.*

He stopped reading for a moment. His wife was a Catholic, coming as she did from Abbeyleix, south of Dublin. They had met at a dance one Sunday night at the local church - he didn't drink then - and quickly hit it off. She had come across to England to work for a doctor in Hyde as a scullery maid and, with her lively intelligence, had soon progressed to running the household. Of course, she stopped working when they got married. The children came along soon afterwards and before he knew it he was buying a house and settling down. That was life, he supposed, something that was never completely planned but just seemed to happen.

He continued reading the letter, hearing her voice as if she were reading it aloud to him.

*Mrs Higgins' son has joined up. He went down one Saturday night to the music hall and they were having one of those recruitment drives. Next minute, he was up on stage signing on for the Lancashire Fusiliers. She's glad he's going now, otherwise he might miss out on the fighting and then he'd regret it for the rest of his life, wouldn't he?*

*I hope you like the scarf I knitted. Sorry about the grey, it was the only wool I had left over after making Hetty's jumper. I hope it keeps you warm. According to the papers it can be cold in Flanders at this time of the year. But I'm sure it can't be as cold as that time we walked up the Cloud and were caught in the rain, do you remember?*

He remembered it so well. The Cloud was a prominent hill a couple of miles south of Macclesfield, near Congleton. They had gone for a day out when they were courting. He had borrowed a couple of bicycles and she had made a picnic hamper of cheese, bread, a few apples and a couple of bottles of Bass pale ale. She didn't approve of drinking, but thought a couple of bottles were a man's right on a Sunday afternoon. They had pedalled to the top of the hill, with its views over Cheshire down below, when a squall of rain had come over and soaked them both. He remembered holding her close as they sheltered beneath the rowan tree, feeling the heat from her body and smelling the strange heady mix of damp and sweet perfume off her clothes.

They were married soon afterwards.

He returned to the letter as another Very light rose into the night.

49

*Jack Davies has asked again about your allotment. He wants to take over the bit where it backs on to his to grow his carrots. I said I would ask you, but I don't like the man. He wants to increase the size of his allotment at your expense. He's been angling after that bit of land for years. Shall I tell him to wait until you get home? It can't be long now, you've been gone over three months and they all said it would be over by Christmas.*

*John, Alice and Hetty all miss you. Hetty is doing well at school and Mr Flowers said she could do really well if she knuckled down. She's started writing and reading now, and I'm sure her letters will be much better than mine very soon.*

*Anyway, look after yourself, dear. You don't know how much I miss you. Life just isn't the same. Write soon and tell me how you are and if you need anything.*

*If I don't hear from you, Merry Christmas. I hope you can come home in 1915.*

*Your loving wife,*
*Norah*

He slowly folded the paper up and placed it back in his top pocket. As he did so, a bullet whined over his head, thudding into the trench support behind him, sending splinters of wood shooting into the night. He ducked instinctively, but far too late to have made any difference if the bullet had hit him.

After a few seconds, a voice shouted from the left: 'Keep your head down, Tommy. Next time, I take it off.'

'Up yours, Fritz,' Tom shouted back, ducking beneath the parapet as another Very light arced into the night sky.

'English wit, Tommy, I remember it well.'

He looked through the trench periscope, desperately searching for the hiding place of the sniper, but couldn't see it.

'You couldn't hit a barn door, Fritz.'

He peered over the top of the parapet, half expecting another bullet to come whizzing towards him.

Nothing. Only another shout, this time further away, off to the right.

'Merry Christmas to you, Tommy. No killing tonight, not tonight.'

There he was, inching his way across no-man's-land, heading back towards the German trenches: a lone sniper.

Tom Wright picked up his Lee Enfield and sighted down the barrel at the retreating figure. He breathed in, taking first pressure on the trigger as he had been taught in training, following the man as he edged slowly away, the sights tracking him as he crawled back towards the German trenches.

Tom fired.

The recoil of the Lee Enfield kicked hard into his shoulder and the bullet struck the earth just in front of the sniper. The man froze in no-man's-land.

Another Very light lit up the sky, revealing the sniper's face as he turned to look back at Tom.

'Merry Christmas to you too, Fritz,' he shouted back, lifting the rifle so it cradled in the crook of his elbow.

The German sniper nodded once and resumed his slow crawl back to the safety of his line.

Tom watched for a while until the man slid noiselessly from view.

Alone in his observation post, he stared out across no-man's-land and listened to the sounds of war.

In the distance, the rumble of artillery. Closer, the pop of the Very lights as they were fired, rising into the sky before exploding in a blaze of light. Closer still, the snores of the men lying in the dugouts or propped against the side of the trench.

One more hour to go and he could sleep.

Blessed sleep.

He missed his family so much.

# Chapter Nine

Friday, December 22, 2017
Didsbury, Manchester

Jayne opened the email from David Wright thirty minutes later. Just enough time for her to indulge in one of her favourite chocolates: a single estate Valrhona from Loma Sotavento in the Dominican Republic. Along with wine, it was her indulgence. And at the moment, she needed the comfort of chocolate.

Snapping off another square, she scanned the email.

*Dear Mrs Sinclair,*

*Thanks for agreeing to help us. You don't know how much it means to me, Martin and Chris.*

*I'm afraid I can't produce much in the way of family history. I didn't know my grandfather very well.*

*I remember him bouncing me on his knee and wearing a silly hat. Perhaps it was my birthday or Christmas, but it will have been the year he died, 1976. I was only three years old then.*

*My dad didn't talk too much about the past - I don't think he knew anything - and besides, he wasn't much bothered about it. He died when I was in my twenties, a heart attack on his way to work at the Post Office. I never thought to ask Mum about the family before she died. You never do, do you? And by the time you think to ask, it's always too late.*

For a second, Jayne looked away from the computer. That's exactly what Robert had said to her not so long ago.

'You'd better ask me about your dad soon, Jayne, I won't be here for ever,' he'd said.

For years she had put off researching her own family history, particularly that of her father. After he had walked out on her and her mother she had never heard from him again.

Was he dead or alive? She didn't know. For a long time, she didn't care. The anger and resentment at him was stronger than any desire to know about her own background. With Robert now lying in hospital, she realised how foolish she had been. If he died, she would never know. He was the last of that generation, the last person to know who her father really was.

At that moment, she made herself a promise. If Robert pulled through this, she would ask him everything. It was time to do what she counselled all her clients to do: face up to the secrets of the past.

She turned back to the email and carried on reading.

*Anyway, here are the details I do know about my dad's side:*

*My father, Anthony Wright, born Stalybridge in 1936, died Sale, Manchester in 1996.*

*My mother, Jane Brennan, born Knock, Ireland in 1938, died December 12, 2017.*

*(My father was the only son as my grandmother died during the war, I was told, and my grandfather never married again.)*

*My grandfather, Tom Wright, born Stalybridge around 1910, died in Sale in 1976.*

*My grandmother Doris Wainwright, born Stalybridge around 1912, died Stalybridge some time in the war.*

*My great-grandfather and great-grandmother both un-known.*

*Sorry, I have nothing more than this. Not much, I'm afraid. I wonder if my grandfather is the Tom Wright on the label, or does it go back even further? The writing is strange. Maybe it's older?*

*I do know my grandfather spent most of his life living in Stalybridge but moved to live with us in Sale when he was old. Dad told me he worked in a mill when he was young and when that closed he ended up as a postman. My dad followed in his footsteps (literally).*

*Sorry, I don't know more, but 1 hope this helps.*

*Best regards,*
*David, Martin and Chris*

Not much to go on, thought Jayne. Nevertheless, it was a start, and as long as she had that she could begin the research. At least she had a name and a place.

Genealogy wasn't rocket science, it was a logical progression of steps to reveal a family's antecedents and forbears. There was a little bit of an art to it - those leaps of faith that helped jump over a wall, or a lack of information. But she tried to avoid those as much as possible, preferring the tried and true methods of empirical research – if it wasn't documented, it didn't exist. Unless she found a piece of paper confirming a theory, for her any guesswork was simply a hypothesis that was being tested.

She decided to start at the beginning, which was actually the end: the death of David's grandfather. She first checked the registration district for Sale. In 1974, it had moved – along with many others in a local government reorganization – from Bucklow to Trafford Registration District. She went to the Free-

BMD site and typed in the name, year and registration location.

*Thomas Wright, 1976. Trafford.*

The website seemed to be working slowly but eventually it came back with a result.

*No records.*

Bugger, thought Jayne.

Then she tried again with an alternative Christian name: Tom.

Still no results.

Unfortunately, Wright was quite a common surname. She removed the Christian name, leaving just the surname, and crossed her fingers. The results could be a few or hundreds.

Six results came back for 1976.

| | Deaths Mar 1976 | | | | |
|---|---|---|---|---|---|
| Surname | First name(s) | DoB | District | Vol | Page |
| Wright | Robert Thomas | 26NO1909 | Trafford | 39 | 2664 |

| | Deaths Jun 1976 | | | | |
|---|---|---|---|---|---|
| Wright | Stephen | 15OC1952 | Trafford | 39 | 1974 |
| Wright | Emily | 17OC1896 | Trafford | 39 | 1998 |

| | Deaths Dec 1976 | | | | |
|---|---|---|---|---|---|
| Wright | Fiona | 10NO1898 | Trafford | 39 | 1990 |
| Wright | Margaret | 21SE1911 | Trafford | 39 | 1873 |
| Wright | John Thomas | 20FE1911 | Trafford | 39 | 2066 |

This was the part of the research that she loved – digging into the past to find the truth from mere snippets of information. She immediately discounted the three named women and the man who was born in 1952. That left her with two results, neither of which matched a 1910 birth date, but that wasn't unusual. People were often forgetful of exact dates of birth and their relatives even more unsure.

Both results had the middle name of Thomas. She had two options:

Robert Thomas Wright or John Thomas Wright.

Which one was David's grandfather?

# Chapter Ten

Thursday, December 24, 1914 – Christmas Eve
Wulverghem, Belgium

The next morning's dawn revealed a beautifully
clear, eggshell blue sky with just a few lazy clouds
slowly meandering from east to west.

Bert had woken first. In fact, he hadn't slept, relieving Harry at four o'clock and staying at post three
until 8.00 a.m. even though he was supposed to have
been replaced much earlier.

The fire in the brazier was burning nicely as the
tea stewed in its pan. Tom stumbled out from the
shallow dugout carved into the clay, stamping his feet
on the frosty covered ground, mist billowing from his
mouth with every word he spoke.

'Nippy out, Bert.'

'Get away, a bit of frost never hurt nobody.'

Tom sat down on an orange create next to the
sergeant, warming his hands on the fire. 'All quiet?'

Bert nodded back towards the German lines.
'Some noise this morning, but I think it was just their
snap being brought up.'

'Anything for us yet?'

Bert pulled back a cloth covering a metal tray.

'Rissoles? Where'd you get them?'

'Saw the cook going up to C Company and
thought I'd have a word. Old mate of mine, is
Charlie. C Company won't miss these.'

Like a bloodhound on the trail of a scent, Harry came stamping out of the dugout. "Owt to eat? Starving, me. Could eat an 'orse.'

Bert looked at the rissoles. 'You may have to.'

'Where'd you get them?'

'Long story,' said Bert, handing one each to Harry and Tom.

Tom took a bite of the bully beef and potatoes, which had been fried in bacon fat. They were still warm and oily, the strands of beef wheedling their way into the gaps between his teeth.

'Good grub, that is,' said Harry, finishing the last of his rissole. 'Any more?'

Bert shook his head. 'Only gave me one each for the platoon, but I managed to snaffle these from him.' From beneath his jacket, Bert produced three small, round and perfectly formed oranges. 'They were for the hofficers, but what they don't have, they won't miss.'

'Never had one of those,' said Harry. 'What they taste like?'

'You've never had an orange?'

'Don't get many in Angel Meadows. Had a banana once. Nicked it from a grocer's. Didn't like it too much, the skin was tough.'

'You're supposed to eat them without the skin, Harry.'

'How was I to know? Didn't come with instructions, did it?'

'Anyway, you peel this too.'

Tom dug his nail into the orange and began to peel back the skin. 'Use this later in the rum, adds a lovely tang to it.'

Bert looked up. 'Now why would you be spoiling good rum with the skin of an orange?'

'We gonna get some rum then?' said Harry.

'We always gets rum at Christmas. Army tradition. Hofficers get whisky and we gets rum.'

'Well, where is it?'

Bert kicked the jar at his feet. Stencilled on it in black were the letters SRD. The jar wobbled slowly before falling over, empty.

Bert shrugged his shoulders. 'Seldom Reaches Destination.'

'Soon Runs Dry,' added Harry.

'Soldier's Rum Disaster,' added Tom.

'At least we've had some breakfast,' finished Bert. 'And a brew of tea.'

Harry and Tom held out their tin mugs. The thick stewed tea was poured from the saucepan. Both men took long draughts of the warming liquid.

'Grows hairs on your chest, that stuff does,' said Harry.

'Grows 'em on the inside of your throat too,' mumbled Tom.

Bert threw his hands up. 'You know I like my tea stewed. Can't stand it when it's weak and milky.'

'You can stand a spoon up in it. How much tea did you use? Hope you saved some for later.'

Bert didn't answer.

They were all quiet for a few minutes, sipping their tea and enjoying the moment to themselves. Luckily, the rest of the platoon was also eating their rissoles and, for those brave enough, washing it down with Bert's tea.

Tom lifted his face to the blue sky, letting the sunshine bathe his tired skin. He felt the light caressing his face – not warming the skin, but illuminating it. For a second, he felt at peace, at ease.

Harry spoke up, destroying the moment. 'You know, if we weren't sitting in the bottom of a muddy trench, if this wasn't the army and we weren't in the arse-end of the world, if Fritz wasn't a hundred yards away with a bloody machine gun trying to kill us, and if we weren't constantly being bossed around by a load of stupid officers, this could be quite a nice place to be. Just sayin', like.'

Nobody answered him as they thought about what he said.

'Need to have a few women, though. Can't do without the women,' Harry added as an afterthought.

'And a nice pint of Bass,' said Bert.

'And the wife and kids,' said Tom.

# Chapter Eleven

Friday, December 22, 2017
Didsbury, Manchester

Jayne stared at the two options for David Wright's grandfather.

As both men were born before 1917, she could order pdf copies of their birth certificates online, checking if either of them were born in Stalybridge.

But before she did that, she decided to check two other records to see if she could narrow down her search. First would be the 1939 register. This was a list of all the people who had been living in the United Kingdom, compiled by the government in the early days of World War Two.

She logged on to Findmypast and entered the information she had on Robert Thomas Wright, including the town of Stalybridge.

No records.

That was a bit worrying. She hoped David had his facts correct. If the town wasn't Stalybridge then she would have to broaden the search to the whole of the UK.

She went over to the shelf in the corner. In most kitchens, the shelves were full of cookbooks; in Jayne's it contained all the research materials for her genealogy work. She pulled the latest edition of the Oxford Dictionary of Family Names in Britain and

Ireland down from its place in the middle of her shelf.

Damn.

According to the University of the West of England, Wright was the thirteenth most popular name in the United Kingdom, with approximately 130,000 people bearing the surname.

Crossing her fingers, she returned to her computer. She entered the details of the second Wright entry and the town in the search field and pressed enter.

A rainbow-coloured wheel took ages to provide her with an answer.

'Bingo,' she shouted out loud. The cat turned to stare at her, then went back to the far more important chore of licking his paws.

| 7 | M o t t r a m Lane | John Thomas | Wright | M | 20Feb11 | M | Postman |
|---|---|---|---|---|---|---|---|
| | | Doris | Wright | F | 04Oct13 | F | House |
| | | XXXXXXXXXXXXXXXXXXXXXXXXXXXXXXX | | | | | |
| | | XXXXXXXXXXXXXXXXXXXXXXXXXXXXXXX | | | | | |

The surnames and Christian names matched David's information. A single row was blanked out, indicating that somebody else was living in the house whose name couldn't be identified as they were born after 1917. This was probably David's father, Anthony, who would have been a child of three when the register was gathered.

Feeling confident she had the right person, Jayne decided it was time to go even further back. Before she started work, she slipped another square of chocolate into her mouth and checked her mobile phone.

No calls.

She hoped that no news from Vera was good news, certain that if Robert's condition had changed in any way, she was sure Vera would have called her immediately.

Jayne went back to her computer. At least when she was working on research, her mind was so focused she had no time to think of her father lying in a hospital bed.

Time to go back to 1911, and even further if she could. She clicked on the website for Findmypast and pulled up the 1911 census, typing the name 'John Thomas Wright' into the search box. This particular census had been taken on April 2 of that year, so if he was born in February, he should appear in the returns.

Unless he was born in a workhouse, then sometimes only the initials of the inmates appeared. It was strange: the late Edwardian workhouses had such a stigma attached to them that census officials didn't even record the names of the inmates.

She pressed enter and almost immediately an answer popped up. She opened the result. A single page from the census appeared on her screen, all the information handwritten in a florid Edwardian style, complete with curlicues and flourishes.

| Thomas Wright | Head | 25 | Married | Piecer | Stalybridge |
| Norah Wright | Wife | 24 | Married | House | Ireland |
| Hetty Wright | Dau | 4 | Single | Student | Stalybridge |
| JohnThomas Wright | Son | 2/12 | Single | | Stalybridge |

The address was listed as 22 Elgin Street. Where had she seen that before? Was it on the label that David Wright and his children had found? She would have to check when she saw him.

But she was pretty sure this was the correct family. The name, year of birth and town all matched. Even if there were more than one Wright in Stalybridge, it would be unlikely that both would have a son called John Thomas.

Jayne brushed her blonde hair away from her eyes. 'So David's great-grandfather was also called Thomas. I wonder if it was cut short to Tom?' she said out loud.

The only reply she received was a loud miaow from Mr Smith. He was now sitting in front of the patio doors, his tail tracing a lazy letter 's' on the floor.

'It's cold, are you sure you want to go out? Is it down to number nine again for dessert, or off to number twenty-seven for a quick dalliance with the ginger moggy?'

There was no answer, only a quick stroke of the glass with a white paw.

She yawned, stretched and got up to open the patio door. The night air was cold, with more than a hint of frost in the air. Immediately, the cat squeezed out and vanished into the dark of the night.

'Enjoy yourself. I'll leave the light on,' she shouted after him, realising straight away how strange this might sound to her neighbours.

She closed the door, shutting out the December cold. The clock on the kitchen wall now read 10.30 p.m. Should she ring Vera to check on Robert? But the sound of Vera's phone ringing might wake him up...

She took three deep breaths, deciding to wait until morning before calling. She must stop worrying. Vera knew exactly what to do – hadn't she spent twenty years working as a nurse?

The ache of tiredness numbed Jayne's eyes. She'd done enough research for tonight. At least she would have something to tell David when they met tomorrow morning.

Her body felt tired, dog-tired. The stresses of today must have affected her even more than she guessed.

As she leant in to switch off her computer, she stared at the census form from 1911.

That handwriting, it looked familiar – as if she had seen it before.

Then she shook her head. Can't be. The census was taken over a hundred years ago. She couldn't recognise the handwriting, could she?

## Chapter Twelve

Thursday, December 24th, 1914 – Christmas Eve
Wulverghem, Belgium

Tom tightened the new grey scarf around his
neck and pulled up the collar of his old overcoat. The
tips of his ears were tingling with the cold. Stomping
his feet did little good, but at least he could still feel
them in the army boots.

He stared out over no-man's-land. The sun was
starting to set behind him, throwing the wire and the
corpses lying across it into shadow.

Only thirty minutes left on this watch. With a bit
of luck they would bring up some hot grub, a nice
cup of cocoa and a tot of rum to warm him up. Then
he would find somewhere dry to get his head down
until his next watch.

'Merry bloody Christmas, Tom,' he whispered,
watching his breath form misty clouds as it came out
of his mouth. It was going to be cold tonight, perhaps the coldest night of the year.

He wondered what Norah was doing back in Stalybridge. Probably tucking the children into their
beds. Hetty and John sleeping in the same room, with
Alice being cradled by her mother, ever ready to
provide a midnight feed. Or now that he wasn't there,
maybe all the children slept with their mother in the
big bed? It wouldn't surprise him.

Perhaps she was reading the catechism. Hetty would be having her first holy communion in the spring and his wife wanted to make sure their daughter was properly prepared, attending the special classes run by Father McNamara on Saturday morning before confession.

Usually, after the children had gone to bed on Christmas Eve, he would sit down and have a glass of pale ale while his wife set out trays of nuts and homemade biscuits and started preparing the goose. Later, she would go to Midnight Mass while he stayed at home to guard over the sleeping children. One day, they would all go together.

He looked up, checking the frost-rimed turnip field that was their only defence against Fritz. Off to the left, the solid crump, crump, crump of artillery. He didn't know if it was theirs or the enemy's and he didn't care. At least the shells weren't landing anywhere near their lines.

Bending down to gaze through the periscope, he scanned the German lines two hundred yards away. In the gathering gloom, the wire in front of their line was like the long branches of a hawthorn tree, most of its leaves blown away by the winds of autumn with just a few ragged spikes remaining.

He laughed to himself. The only thing they were blown away by was the shells of the 7.5s.

They had received a new batch of men from Blighty this morning – 450 bodies to finally bring the battalion back up to strength. He felt sorry for the poor sods. Fancy being told you have to leave England in the week before Christmas and then arriving at the billets behind the front lines on Christmas Eve. No doubt they would come into the line to relieve them soon, tasting the joys of life in the trenches for the first time.

Happy New Year, lads.

He heard a noise coming from the German lines, like a rustling sound.

Another raiding party? Surely the Germans wouldn't try it on Christmas Eve?

He gazed out through the periscope. Something was happening on the enemy line in front of him. He could sense, but could not see, a hint of movement going from the left, and carrying on through their trench.

Were they reinforcing for an attack? But there had been no artillery bombardment.

'Oi, Bert,' he whispered to his sergeant, who was sleeping beside the brazier. 'Summat's up.'

'Whazzat?' Bert woke with a start. 'Whassup?'

'Something's happening in the German line.'

Bert was on his feet and beside Tom Wright in seconds, staring through the periscope. 'Summat's going up along their line.'

'Are they going to attack?'

'Dunno. But I can see one of the Germans with his head above their trench. He's carrying something.'

Tom sighted down the barrel of his Lee Enfield, following the direction in which Bert had pointed.

'I can see him. Shall I shoot?'

Bert touched his shoulder. ''Ang on a minute, I'll get the hofficer.'

As ever, Bert wouldn't take a shit without the go-ahead from above.

Captain Lawson arrived a minute later.

'What's going on, Wright?'

'There's more of them now, sir. I've counted five of them out of their line. They seem to be putting trees on top of their trenches.'

'Don't be daft, man. It must be some sort of weapon. Sergeant?'

'Yes, sir.' Bert was right next to him.

'Wake your men and get them into their firing positions.'

'Yes, sir,' he answered loudly.

'But do it quietly.'

'Yes, sir,' he whispered.

Captain Lawson bent down and peered through the periscope, sweeping the German line from left to right. 'They are putting something on the parapets of their trenches. I can't see what it is.'

Captain Lawson's batman handed him a pair of the latest stereo prism binoculars from Ross in London.

He put them to his eyes and said, 'Well, I'll be blowed.'

## Chapter Thirteen

Thursday, December 24th, 1914 – Christmas Eve
Wulverghem, Belgium

They were still all at their firing posts, staring across no-man's-land at the German lines.

On the parapets of the trenches opposite, a row of five-feet-tall Christmas trees had been placed. Men were standing beside them lighting candles and carefully placing them in the branches.

Bert and Harry were next to Tom on the firing step of post three, their rifles still pointed forward towards the Germans. Captain Lawson had run back to the command post to report in.

'Rum do, this,' said Bert.

Harry stared across at him. 'Speaking of rum—'

'It's not come up yet. Looks like it won't tonight,' interrupted Bert.

'You'd think the one thing the bloody Army could get right was to give a man a drink at Christmas. I mean, it's the one enjoyment in life the working man has, right?'

Neither of the others bothered to answer him.

The sky was gradually growing darker behind them, making the flickering light of the candles in the Christmas trees seem brighter, more luminescent.

Tom could see the unshaven face of one of the Germans as it was lit up first by the orange flame of his lighter, followed by the softer, yellow light of the candle.

Captain Lawson returned and stood next to him.

'We're to keep watching them and report back if there are any developments.'

'What do you make of it, sir?'

The officer scratched his head through his peaked cap. 'I don't rightly know. It looks like they are celebrating Christmas.'

One by one the Germans jumped back in their trenches, leaving the Christmas trees and their flickering lights like a small forest growing out of the strands of barbed wire.

Only one German was left. He shouted, 'Thank you for not firing, Tommy,' in heavily accented English.

Tom recognised the voice of the sniper from last night. 'It's okay,' he shouted back, 'we're saving our bullets for later.'

The man vanished from sight as he jumped down into his trench.

Captain Lawson scanned the German line through his binoculars once more. 'I think you can stand the men down, Sergeant, but ask them to keep their rifles handy in case it's a ruse.'

'Yes, sir.' Bert ran down the line of the trench, telling the men to step down. Grumbling, they all returned to gather around their warm braziers or lie on the straw in a dugout for the night.

Tom was relieved at post three by a young squaddie from Stockport and went back to sitting on his rickety orange crate, warming his frozen hands on the fire.

'Still no rum?' asked Harry.

'Shut up about the bloody rum. If it ain't come up by now, it ain't never coming up.'

As Bert finished his sentence, a Quartermaster Sergeant appeared at the end of the trench carrying a large pan of steaming cocoa, accompanied by a young soldier with a stone jar of rum with the black letters 'SPD' stencilled on the side.

Harry rubbed his hands. 'Speak of the devil.' He rummaged in his kit bag to find his metal cup for the cocoa.

The QM Sergeant finally got to them after twenty minutes.

'Thought you'd never get here,' said Harry, holding out his tin cup.

The sergeant ladled the hot, steaming cocoa into it, filling up Tom and Bert's cups next.

The young soldier with the stone jar was standing next to his sergeant.

'Time for my rum.' Harry put his cocoa down and took a small empty glass from the young soldier. 'Don't tell me you've run out.'

The QM Sergeant smiled. 'We've run out. Your mates back there had the last drop.'

'Would you believe it? The bloody army couldn't organise a bloody piss-up in a bloody brewery.'

The QM Sergeant smiled again. 'Just kidding. It's double rations tonight, courtesy of the bloody army.'

The young soldier poured a double tot into the glass, which was greedily swallowed by Harry. 'That tickled the throat,' he said, wiping his mouth. 'Couldn't have more, could I?'

'Sorry, Oliver Twist, got the rest of your company to go round.'

The young soldier handed Bert and Tom their rum rations, before moving on to the next brazier.

'I'll sleep well tonight...'

'Shush, what's that?' Tom pulled his scarf away from his ears. 'Hear it?'

The others listened too.

'It sounds like singing, coming from the German trenches, I think.'

The rest of the men, including the QM Sergeant, had stopped what they were doing and were all listening.

The song became clearer and louder, carried across no man's land on a gentle breeze.

*Stille Nacht! Heilige Nacht!*
*Alles schläft. Eynsam wacht*
*Nur das traute heilige Paar.*
*Holder Knab' im lockigten Haar,*
*Schlafe in himmlischer Ruh!*

*Stille Nacht! Heilige Nacht!*
*Gottes Sohn! O! wie lacht*
*Lieb' aus deinem göttlichen Mund,*
*Da uns schlägt die rettende Stund.*
*Jesus! in deiner Geburt!*

'They're singing *Silent Night*,' said Bert, 'only the words are strange.'

'It's German,' answered Tom. 'They're singing the carol in German. I heard it once sung by a woman at our church in Stalybridge. She was from Bavaria, I remember.'

The whole trench was silent now, each man listening to the words and tune of the carol as it drifted over the mud, slime and rusted barbed wire between the two lines.

Finally, the song came to a beautiful end, with the repeated last phrase.

*Jesus der Retter ist da!*
*Jesus der Retter ist da!*

A few seconds later, a voice shouted from their lines. 'It's your turn, Tommy.'

'What's that, Fritz?'

'It's your turn to sing, Tommy.'

All the men from the platoon were staring at Tom. He tried hard to remember the words, then began singing, hesitantly and a little off-key at first.

*'Silent night! Holy night! All is calm, all is bright...'*

His voice became stronger as he remembered more and more of the words. Gradually, the other men joined in. Particularly loud was the QM Sergeant, who had a fine baritone.

*Round yon Virgin Mother and Child!*
*Holy Infant, so tender and mild,*
*Sleep in heavenly peace!*
*Sleep in heavenly peace!*

It was the Sergeant who continued when Tom couldn't remember the second verse.

*Silent night! Holy night!*
*Shepherds quake at the sight!*
*Glories stream from Heaven afar,*
*Heavenly Hosts sing Alleluia!*
*Christ the Saviour is born!*
*Christ the Saviour is born!*

After the last repeated line, the men stopped singing and turned to each other, laughing.

From across no-man's-land, the sound of clapping and cheering, followed by the same German voice as before. 'Not bad, Tommies, not bad.'

A few seconds later, another Christmas carol rang out from the German trenches, this time louder, with more voices.

*O Tannenbaum, o Tannenbaum*
*Wie treu sind deine Blatter*
*Du grünst nicht nur zur Sommerzeit,*
*Nein, auch im Winter, wenn es schneit.*
*O Tannenbaum, o Tannenbaum,*
*Wie treu sind deine Blätter.*

*O Tannenbaum, o Tannenbaum,*
*Du kannst mir sehr gefallen.*
*Wie oft hat nicht zur Weihnachtszeit*
*Ein Baum von dir mich hoch erfreut.*
*O Tannenbaum, o Tannenbaum,*
*Du kannst mir sehr gefallen.*

This time the end of their carol was followed by cheers and clapping from the British side. The applause had barely ended before the QM Sergeant began singing in his deep baritone.

*O come, all ye faithful,*
*Joyful and triumphant!*
*O come ye, o come ye to Bethlehem.*
*Come and behold Him,*
*Born the King of Angels!*
*O come, let us adore Him*
*O come, let us adore Him*
*O come, let us adore Him*
*Christ the Lord!*

All the men joined in, singing at the top of their voices, making sure their song was heard in the trenches opposite.

When they had finished, there was another round of applause in the distance, followed by a melody they had heard before.

Bert grabbed Tom's arm. 'They's singing the National Anthem. Are you sure they're German?'

Tom listened.

*Heil dir im Siegerkranz,*
*Herrscher des Vaterlands!*
*Heil, Kaiser, dir!*
*Fühl in des Thrones Glanz*
*Die hohe Wonne ganz,*
*Liebling des Volks zu sein!*
*Heil Kaiser, dir!*

'The words sound German.'

'It's a German song, basically saying how wonderful the Kaiser is.' It was Captain Lawson speaking. He had managed to creep up on them silently again. 'A very nationalistic song.'

'Really?' said Harry. 'I'll give them a song for their wonderful Kaiser.'

He immediately began singing.

*Four-and-twenty virgins come down from Inverness,*
*And when the Ball was over,*
*There were four-and-twenty less,*
*Singin' balls to your partner, your ass against the wall,*
*If ya never been had on a Saturday night,*
*Ya never been had at all!*

All the other men joined in except the QM Sergeant, who looked on, red-faced.

*There was doin' in the parlour,*
*There was doin' on the stones,*

*But ya couldn't hear the music for the wheezin' and the groans,*
*Singin' balls to your partner, your ass against the wall,*
*If ya never been had on a Saturday night,*
*Ya never been had at all!*

*The undertaker, he was there,*
*All wrapped up in a shroud,*
*Swingin' from the chandelier and peein' on the crowd...*

This time there were cheers from the Germans. 'It's the British sense of humour, Tommy, yes?'

'Aye,' Harry shouted back, 'and balls to the Kaiser!'

'And balls to King George,' came the answer.

Harry was about to shout again when his arm was grabbed by Captain Lawson.

'That's enough, Larkin.'

'But sir—'

Before Harry could continue, another chorus of *Silent Night* came from the German trenches.

Soon the Cheshires joined in, led by the QM Sergeant and even including Captain Lawson this time.

Tom looked up at the clear night sky. The moon was full, shining down on the hard frosted ground between the two trenches. Stars twinkled in the sky as they had done for millennia. Occasionally, a cloud, late for some meeting, scudded across the sky.

For once, no Very lights lit up the night with their floating luminescence and the thunder and lightning of artillery was missing, away on leave.

He could hear the words of the carol - German on one side and English on the other - flowing back and forth across no-man's-land, dodging the wire and the dead bodies.

Finally, the singing from both sides ended.

Silence.

Not a sound from either trench.

A single voice came from the German side. 'Merry Christmas, Tommy.'

Tom cupped his mouth with his hands and shouted back. 'Merry Christmas, Fritz.'

Then he lapsed into silence, as did the rest of the men.

Across no-man's-land, the German trenches were quiet too.

It was a silent night, a holy night.

# Chapter Fourteen

Saturday, December 23, 2017
Didsbury, Manchester

Jayne was up early the next morning, messaging Vera immediately to check if her father had spent a comfortable night.

**How is he?**

Whilst she was waiting for the answer, she popped a capsule in the coffee machine.

In the middle of the night, she had woken up with a start, suddenly aware where she had seen the handwriting on the census form. It was obvious once she thought about it.

She took the small espresso and opened the patio door to let Mr Smith back in the house, inhaling the fresh air of a bright December morning mixed with the strong aroma of the coffee. The cat wasn't in his usual place, waiting on the step, so she softly called his name.

In the light from the kitchen, she could see her small lawn had a dusting of frost on the tips of the grass and the leaves of her roses were jewelled with drops of frozen ice. They reflected the light back at her, like so many diamonds glittering.

She stood there for a few moments, taking it all in before she heard Mr Smith hustle over the top of the fence, leap across the lawn and dart through her legs into the kitchen.

'Good morning. Enjoyed your night on the tiles, did we? I suppose you're hungry?'

A miaow came back from the direction of his bowl.

'Have to be dry cat food again, I'm afraid. Beggars can't be choosers.'

She filled up his bowl with his least favourite food and, before she had even stepped back, his head was rammed down, crunching away.

'Obviously you've been working up an appetite.'

She brewed another coffee, inhaling the pleasant aroma. What was it about coffee and mornings? It was as if the two were inseparable for her. Like Laurel and Hardy. Or ham and eggs. Or Holmes and Watson. 'Coffee and Sinclair,' she said out loud. 'It has a certain ring to it.'

As she sat down at her computer, she realised she was in a strange, almost euphoric mood. Was it a reaction to her father being in hospital? People react in the strangest ways to stress. For her, it made her feel almost light-headed.

There was an antidote, though.

Work.

She switched on the computer, determined to trace more details of David Wright's family. Could she go further back? In those days, there was less population movement than now. Thomas Wright, the great-grandfather, had probably been born and bred in Stalybridge.

If she could find his father on the 1881 census, the Lost Cousins site would be able help David to find links to possible relatives he knew nothing about.

It would be her Christmas gift to him, and to his son in hospital.

As she started work, the phone buzzed with Vera's reply.

**Fine. He slept all night. The doctor will look over him again at 8 am.**

Jayne answered immediately.

**That's great news. I'll be there at noon to take over.**

**Don't worry, take your time. See you then. Love Vera.**

She was lucky to have such a wonderful step-mother. A woman who made Robert so very happy.

Please let him get well so they can enjoy their time together as man and wife.

Jayne wasn't a religious woman but it was the nearest she had come to a prayer.

With worries of her father relieved, it was time to knuckle down to some serious research.

Two hours of solid work later, she had what she wanted. She had traced Thomas Wright through the 1901 and 1891 censuses, discovering that his father, Alfred Wright, also worked as a piecer in a mill.

Working in the factory was obviously a family affair, with jobs handed from father to son. Thomas was the youngest boy of a family of seven, born in 1886.

She would show David how to trace his family using Lost Cousins. If he did, he would be able to contact distant relatives – perhaps discover photos, stories or memories that would help him piece together the family history.

She checked the clock: 8.30 a.m. Time to get ready. She printed out everything she had discovered and put it all in a folder for David, keeping the census form from 1911 on top. That was her most important discovery.

She threw on a pair of jeans and a jumper, tied her hair back in a ponytail and ran out of the house, grabbing her papers and laptop. Mr Smith, dozing on the windowsill beside the door, didn't even raise his head as she ran past.

The traffic was horrendous, of course, it was a couple of days before Christmas. She was fifteen minutes late when she arrived at David Wright's house near Heaton Park.

He was waiting for her outside with his son Martin.

'It's Saturday, not playing football today?' she asked the boy, stepping out of her BMW.

'Nah, not while school is off.'

'Lucky you.'

He smiled a lopsided grin.

She shook David's hand. 'I've a lot to show you, but first I'd like to see the label you showed me before.'

Martin reached into the Tesco bag and pulled it out; he had now placed it in a plastic folder.

Jayne studied it for a few seconds. 'I thought so.'

She brought out the printout of the census form for 1911.

'See, the names are the same.'

David Wright frowned. 'The census form says Thomas Wright, and this says Tom Wright.'

Jayne smiled. 'I didn't mean that. Look closely, the handwriting is the same.'

David leant in and so did Martin.

'See the flow of the capital "T", the scrolling tail of the "R" and the way the "ght" at the end of Wright is all joined together in one flowing movement.'

David stared back at her. 'What does it mean?'

'In the 1911 Census people filled in the forms themselves, the enumerator merely checked the details. Luckily, the schedules have survived. This is Tom Wright's handwriting.'

'So if this is his signature, then the writing on the label must have been written by the same man,' said Martin.

'Clever lad,' said Jayne. 'It also means the label belonged first to your great-grandfather not your grandfather. It's older than you think.'

'But what does the number mean? And what about the strange green words on the back?'

'That's what we're about to find out. Want to come with me, Martin?'

# Chapter Fifteen

Saturday, December 23, 2017
Cheetham Hill, Manchester

Jayne pressed the door-bell and stood back, looking up at the second-floor window.

'Are you sure this is the right place?' asked David Wright.

The shop had a hand-painted sign hanging precariously above the door. Herbert Levy & Sons. The door itself was painted a shade of forest green that had obviously once been a job lot from an army paint sale. The walls had a mottled effect, used more often on camouflage pants rather than on brick. In a jungle, the place would have blended in perfectly, but sandwiched between a kosher butchers and a Thai massage parlour, it stood out like a Casanova in a harem.

Martin shielded his eyes and peered through the wire mesh covering the dusty windows. 'It doesn't look like anybody's home.'

'Oh, he's here, just taking a few minutes to tidy up before he opens the door.'

As if by magic, the door swung open as Jayne finished the sentence.

'Inspector Sinclair, what a pleasant surprise. To what do I owe this pleasure?'

The speaker was an aged man who smelt vaguely of cats. He hadn't shaved for at least two weeks and his face was as creased as an old pair of trousers.

Above the sharp blue eyes, two white, hairy caterpillar eyebrows moved independently, neither co-ordinating with the rest of the facial muscles.

'Good morning, Herbert, I hope we didn't wake you. And remember, I'm not police any more.'

Herbert was brilliant at what he did, which, for the most part, was selling dubious antiques. He had crossed Jayne's path more than once in her previous life as a copper when his name had come up as a receiver of stolen goods.

She brushed past him to enter the shop, followed by David and Martin. All three danced their way through a jumble of assorted uniforms, ammo boxes, trench coats, Victorian postcards, dressers, movie posters, horse brasses, stuffed armchairs, fake Tiffany lamps and African assegais.

'I thought you said he was tidying up,' said Martin, picking up a dusty Edwardian vase.

'There's tidying up and then there's Herbert's tidying up. Most people do a spot of dusting or cleaning, but his tidying involves hiding away stuff he doesn't want me to see. Isn't that true, Herbert?'

'I dunno know what you mean, Inspector Sinclair. I've been straight for over five years now. The last stretch in Walton Nick nearly did me in. The money's in decorative items for young puppies these days.' The accent was London, not Manchester, with an affected cockney drawl.

Jayne brushed aside the large frond of an aspidistra standing in front of an old desk.

'I didn't know you were branching out, Herbert? And it's yuppies, not puppies.'

The man squeezed past her to stand behind an old cash register on the desk. Jayne smelt the odour of cats as he went past.

'Business is very good, Inspector. Victorian is very in at the moment.'

'These are cool.' Martin picked up a pair of split-lens flying goggles and put them on his head.

'French. Second World War, they are. They'd make a wonderful Christmas present. For you, only fifty quid. A bargain, even if I do say so myself.'

Martin looked at his father, who shook his head slowly. The young boy returned the goggles to their position on top of a set of antique bibles.

'Let me introduce David Wright and his son, Martin.'

The antique dealer leant over the counter to shake David's hand. 'An electrician, I see. Not working over Christmas?'

David looked shocked. 'How did you—?'

Herbert tapped the side of his nose. 'I got the eye. Same as my old dad.'

Jayne looked at her watch. She wanted to get out to Macclesfield before noon, to see how her father was doing and give Vera a break. 'I've brought David and Martin here because they need your help identifying a few objects.'

Herbert breathed an audible sigh of relief. 'So it's a visit for business, not pleasure, Inspector.'

'I told you, I'm not with the police any more. I do genealogical investigations now.'

'Didn't know you were a doctor too, Mrs Sinclair.'

Jayne shook her head. 'Genealogical investigations, not gynaecological investigations, Herbert. There is a difference. Anyway, can we move on? Martin, please show Mr Levy the objects you found in the trunk.'

The old man brushed a grey hair off his forehead. 'Mister Levy, I like that. Has a certain ring to it.'

Martin reached into the Tesco bag and carefully laid the silver button, the label and the lump of old leather on the dusty counter.

Herbert's eyes lit up and he immediately snatched up the button. With the other hand he slipped a loop out of his pocket and fixed it to his eye.

'Haven't seen one of these for a long time. Not bad condition; brass covered by silver gilt. 35th Landsturm Regiment. World War One, before 1916, I'd say – with a probable date early in the war.'

'This is from the First World War?' asked Jayne.

Herbert nodded. 'German Army. Worth about a hundred quid.' He looked at David. 'Easy to get rid of if you wanna sell.'

'It was in the same chest as these things, Herbert. Do you know what they are?'

The antique dealer picked up the label, turning over both sides and examining the writing under his loop.

'It's a label.'

'We know that.'

'To be precise, it's a label that once was attached to a German tree.'

'How do you know it's German?' asked Jayne.

'My grandparents came here in the thirties, spoke to me in German, didn't they? See the words: Weihnachtsfest Baum. Weihnachtsfest means Christmas, and Baum means tree.'

'It's a Christmas-tree label? Why would my great-grandfather have a German Christmas-tree label?'

Herbert looked behind him. 'You ask me, I ask who?' He turned the label over to show Tom Wright's name in his florid handwriting, the number 12725 and an address in Stalybridge. At the side, and in a different hand from the rest of the writing, were the numbers 3-2.

'Well, that makes it obvious.'

'What makes what obvious, Herbert?' asked Jayne.

'This here Tom Wright – 'e was in the army.'

'My great-granddad was in the German Army?' asked David.

'No,' said Herbert, 'that's a British Army number. An early one too, I think.'

'What about the 3-2?'

Herbert shrugged his shoulders. 'Beats me. I never seen extra numbers like that beside a soldier's army number.'

'So let's get this right. The badge is German?'

'Definitely. The 35th Regiment.'

'The label is German?'

'I think so. The words are German.'

'But it's got the name, address and number of a British soldier – David's great-grandfather – on it? It doesn't make sense.'

Herbert shrugged his shoulders again. 'That's life, Inspector.'

'You're a great help. What about the leather object?'

The antique dealer picked it up and examined it closely. 'Well, it's old, hand-sewn by the look of it. None of that machine crap. See, the stitching is slightly irregular. The leather has seen better days, but with a bit of TLC, it could be brought back to life.' He peered through the lacing into the interior. 'That's interesting, never seen anything like that before.'

'What is it?'

Before he could answer, a young man wearing a black bomber jacket and Dr. Martens bustled into the shop carrying a parcel under his arm.

'Not now, Gerald. I 'ave a customer.'

Gerald looked up, surprised. 'But I've got the stuff you—'

Before he could finish his sentence, Herbert cut him off. 'Not now! I've got a customer. Inspector Sinclair.'

Gerald took one look at Jayne, his mouth opened and he exited the shop as quickly as he had entered.

'You up to your old tricks, Herbert?'

The old man held his hands wide open. 'Me, Inspector? Not on your life. Gerald is my assistant. 'Elps me with the 'ouse clearances, he does. Now, looking at this object...' he said, changing the subject quickly. 'I don't know what it is, but I 'ave a friend who might. Charlie Robinson. Got a good eye, has Charlie.'

'When can you let him see it?'

'I'm at an auction wiv him at noon, so I could call you back this afternoon wiv a result.'

Jayne looked across at David, who nodded.

'Okay, Herbert, we'll leave it with you. But don't let me down. Otherwise a phone call to Duncan Worsley at Cheetham Hill Nick might be needed. I presume you have receipts for all this?' Jayne pointed to all the bric-a-brac cluttering the shop.

'Don't be like that, Mrs Sinclair. I won't let you down. And I'm an honest businessman now. Straight as the proverbial dagger, me.'

Jayne frowned. 'You'd better be, Herbert, otherwise you'll be straight back in the proverbial nick.'

## Chapter Sixteen

Friday, December 25th, 1914 – Christmas Day
Wulverghem, Belgium

Tom Wright woke up stiff, sore and cold. He had
managed to find himself a corner in the dugout
where he sat on some straw and leant against the hard
wooden pillow of a prop. He pulled his coat around
his neck and stomped his feet on the ground to try to
force some life into them.

The slime and mud at the bottom of the trench
had frozen solid after the hard frost last night. Bert
was already in position, sitting on an orange crate with
his hands over the brazier, the coals giving off a
bright orange glow.

'Don't you ever sleep, Bert?' Tom's words came
out as a white mist, like the breath of a dragon.

'Can't see the point. Plenty of time to sleep when
we go back to the billets.'

'You know there isn't. They'll have us spitting and
polishing like it's gone out of style. Last time, you
ended up spending your days painting rocks white.'

'Beats being here, though, don't it?'

Bert had a point. Except this morning, this
Christmas morning, the sky was a bright, bright blue
and the air was as clean and clear as it was on top of
the Cloud.

It would be a lovely day to be alive, thought Tom, if I wasn't in some bloody trench with half the German army only a couple of hundred yards away, desperate to kill us.

'Merry Christmas, lads.' It was Harry, running down the trench, ensuring he kept his head below the parapet.

'You're up early.'

'Found a little nest to sleep in last night, didn't I? Captain Lawson was on duty last night so I bedded down in his dugout.'

'They'd have you shot if they found out, Harry,' said Bert.

'They ain't gonna find out, are they? Had to bung the little batman the fags but it was worth it.'

Bert shook his head.

'Any chance of a cuppa?'

'It's stewing.'

'What you done, put beef in it?'

Bert shook his head. 'Just tea. Bully beef ain't come up yet.'

'What's for breakfast?'

'Same as yesterday,' said Bert.

'What's that?'

'A plate full of hopes and dreams with a dash of disappointment on the side,' answered Tom. 'And when you've finished that, I'll warm up some roast goose with lashings of gravy and roast spuds.'

'They've brought up the dinner already?'

'In your dreams, mate.' Bert handed him a tin cup full of a dark, ochre-coloured liquid. 'Drink your tea.'

'I could eat this with a knife and fork.'

'Hey, Sergeant,' one of the soldiers shouted from post three. 'Summat's up in the German trenches. One of them is standing on his parapet waving his arms.'

Bert rushed over to the periscope and peered into it. The German was standing in full view out of his trench beside the Christmas tree, waving his right arm in the air.

'What's the bugger up to?'

'Shall I kill him, Sergeant?'

'Not yet. Captain Lawson said not to fire on any of them without orders.'

'He's stepping through his wire towards us, shouting something.'

Tom strained to hear what the man was saying.

'Tommy, are you awake yet? Tommy...'

'I can shoot him easy, Sergeant. Sitting duck, he is.'

'Hold it, Blake. I don't want any firing without a hofficer here.' He shouted back over his shoulder: 'Harry, can you find Captain Lawson?'

Tom stuck his head over the top of the parapet. The German was still walking slowly towards them, holding a box in his arms and talking at the same time. 'Let's talk, Tommy. It's Christmas, let's talk.'

Without thinking, Tom put his foot on one of the retaining boards and pushed himself up above the parapet, scrambling up to the top of the trench on his hands and knees.

'What you doing?' shouted Bert.

Tom Wright ignored him and walked out, through the wire, past the dead German draped across it and out into no-man's-land.

'Come back, Tom!'

Bert's voice sounded very far away now.

Tom looked up. The sun shone weakly, trying to break through the haze. Off to the left, a red-breasted robin perched on a tree stump, trilling its welcome to the world. His boots crunched the frozen ground, sending up flecks of frost into the morning air.

The German was only thirty yards away now. He was smaller than Tom; about five feet and five inches, dark haired, unshaven, wearing a dull grey overcoat and a soft hat with a round button in the centre.

They both reached the middle of no-man's-land at the same time.

'Morning, Tommy.' It was the same voice as the sniper from two nights ago. That strange accent; a mixture of Manchester and German, with a touch of cockney thrown in for good measure.

'Morning, Fritz.'

'My name is Harald. Harald Kanz from Leipzig.'

The man stuck his hand out.

# Chapter Seventeen

Saturday, December 23, 2017
Macclesfield General Hospital, Cheshire

Jayne stood in front of Robert's bed in the hospital. Off to the left, the machines were still beeping regularly. His face was peaceful, as if he was in the deepest sleep he had ever experienced. His breathing was regular; a slight rise and fall of the NHS sheet and blanket revealing he was breathing at all.

The doctor had been very positive when he saw Jayne and Vera. 'He's had a good night's rest and the antibiotics seem to be clearing up the chest infection.'

'I can vouch for that,' said Vera. 'He was so quiet all night, I had to get up every five minutes to check.'

'You do know the machines will go off if there is any change in his heart rate or breathing?'

Vera drew herself up to her full five-foot-one-inch of height. She seemed to tower over the doctor. 'I used to be a nurse. I'm quite capable of checking vital signs.'

'I'm very sorry, Mrs Cartwright, we rely on the machines to do it for us these days.'

'There's nothing better than a human touch.'

'So he's getting better, Doctor?' Jayne intervened between the two of them.

'It's still a little bit too early to judge, Mrs Sinclair, but the prognosis is good. We'll know for certain in a couple of days.'

'I hope he can be better before Christmas,' said Vera.

'We all do, Mrs Cartwright. Now, if you'll excuse me, I have other patients to see.'

Vera had stayed for five minutes more, briefing Jayne in excruciating detail of what she had to do if there was any change in Robert's vital signs.

And then she too was gone, back to the retirement home to have a nap and a shower. She would return later. Luckily, Mr Smith had plenty of food in his bowl so Jayne wouldn't have to return to Didsbury that night.

After checking on Robert, which involved simply watching his chest rise in rhythm to the beat from the machine, she sat in the chair opposite his bed and took out her laptop.

The three other beds in the ward were occupied, but as two of the patients were sleeping and the other was listening to the television through his earphones, she had finally found a quiet place to work.

The discoveries this morning were interesting. David's great-grandfather had been a soldier in the British Army fighting in World War One. But why did he have just one German button? She had heard of soldiers bringing back German helmets as souvenirs, but a button? And how did he get hold of it? Surely, a person would take more than one button?

She shook her head. And why did he have the green label? Did it mean something to him? A label for a Christmas tree? And what was the leather object? Was it from the same time, or something completely different? Perhaps it was something they used in the trenches?

These objects must have meant something to Tom Wright, otherwise why keep them safe and secure, wrapped up in the bottom of a chest?

For a second, the hospital ward seemed to blur and slowly dissipate. She found herself looking down on a scar in the ground, where people were stepping up to firing steps, rifles and bayonets pointing forward. A man was walking up and down behind them, shouting.

She couldn't hear what he was saying. What was it? The voice was urgent, excited. She tilted her head but the voice seemed garbled, muffled. She wrinkled her nose. A smell drifted up from the scar in the earth below her. The smell of decomposition, of rotting flesh, of death.

A loud beep from one of her father's machines brought her back to the ward. She stood up and gazed down on Robert. He was still sleeping peacefully, the oxygen mask snug across his nose and mouth.

They didn't often come, these 'moments', as she liked to call them. But ever since she had been a child, they had visited her at the strangest times, usually brought on by a place, a smell or a person. It was like the past had come alive and she was surrounded by it. She was still herself, of course, and still aware, but she was no longer in her own time but transported back to another long-dead one.

Robert had always teased her about it, saying it was just the product of an overzealous imagination. But the moments had remained, still occurring even when she was in the police.

She remembered going to the scene of one particularly grizzly killing in Moss Side. One minute she was standing at the entrance to the door, with scene-of-crime officers walking past her dressed in their white coveralls, the next she was watching and hearing the man attack his wife with a butcher's knife. The blood spurting across the wall, her cries for mercy, his snarls, the grating noise as the knife cut through the skull, snagging on some bone, and his breathless grunts as he tried to pull it out.

It was as if she were with him in the room at the time the crime was committed. Even stranger, when the pathologist produced his report, all the details she had imagined when she had entered the house were written there in black and white, right down to the incisions in the bone of the skull.

She shook her head again. Must concentrate, can't dwell on the past – not now, not here.

She sat down again and reopened her laptop. She had to find out the truth for David, Martin and Chris.

Luckily, they knew the great-grandfather's name and now, thanks to Herbert, his army number.

She logged on to Ancestry.com and accessed the British Army's World War One service records, hoping that Tom Wright was one of the 'burnt records'.

Nearly five million men had served in the British Army in World War One, and as with anything the British undertook, the bureaucracy was meticulous. Unfortunately, in a bombing raid in 1940, over 60 per cent of those records had been destroyed. The ones that survived were called the 'burnt records'.

She entered his name and crossed her fingers. As she waited for the results to come up, she glanced across at Robert, who was still sleeping peacefully in his bed. She knew he was a fighter and prayed he would be able to come through this.

She looked down at her laptop. Over 1600 records had come back. Damn, she had forgotten that Wright was a popular name. She entered the army number from the label, hoping to narrow the choices.

Now it was down to 544 results. They can't all have the same number, can they? Frowning, Jayne opened the first result in the list. A man born in a small town in Essex.

The second listing came from Pontypridd in Wales. The third from Cardiff.

Perhaps this was going to be harder than she thought. She clicked on the fourth result and up popped a Territorial Force Enlistment Form, dated 1912.

She quickly scanned the form. The address was the same as in the census – she had found her man. Handwritten in pencil at the top of the form were his number and his regiment: the Cheshires. Of course, where else would he serve but the force from his own county?

She clicked either side of this record and more results appeared. His documents were obviously some of those that had survived the bombing.

After thirty minutes of going back and forth in the records, courtesy of the haphazard filing of the Army bureaucracy, she was finally able to write a series of notes on Tom Wright's involvement in World War One, with her thoughts in brackets.

*Territorial Army: June 10 1912. Enlisted in the 6th Battalion of Cheshire Regiment for a period of four years.*

*Called up: August 5 1914 (the day after the outbreak of war).*

*November 10 1914: Arrived in France with the 6th Battalion of the Cheshire Regiment.*

*December 17 1914: Attached to 15 Brigade, 5th Division in Flanders.*

*March-December 1915: On guard duty in Rouen and Dieppe.*

*November 1915: Confined to barracks for ten days for being drunk and disorderly.*

*July 30 1916: Shrapnel wound during Battle of the Somme. Southampton General Hospital for twelve days (check hospital records).*

*Returned to duty in Chester, October 6.*
*Rejoined 6th Battalion to France, December 24, 1916.*
*Gunshot wound November 1917. Hospitalised in Manchester. (Which hospital?)*
*Returned to France April 1918.*
*Discharged from duty March 14 1919.*

The bare bones of a soldier's life in the First World War. Tom Wright had been in the army virtually from the first day, surviving until the end of the war, wounded at least twice.

There were three other documents of interest. She was about to take notes on these when a ginger-haired nurse came in to check up on Robert.

'How is he?' she asked as she looked up his medical sheet at the end of the bed.

'Very quiet. Hasn't moved in the hour I've been here.'

'That's great.'

'Not moving is great?'

'The sedative and the antibiotics are working. During this time, it's best if he conserves his strength. Sleep is the great healer. Better than any doctor.'

After checking the other patients in the ward, she bustled out of the door without saying any more.

Jayne stared at Robert. He was so still it was frightening.

'Please make him well. Please.'

She thought about taking a break and getting some coffee but she couldn't bear to leave Robert in case something happened. Instead, she returned to the file on Tom Wright.

The three documents at the end of the packet were the most interesting. A medical examination on his discharge in 1919 described his gunshot wound and its effect:

*Subject complains of constant pain in his left arm following gunshot wound at Passchendaele in November 1917. Can no longer perform work. Examination of arm reveals entrance scar combined with surgical intervention. Scar 3" x 1" across surface, upper third left arm. Healed tissue and puckered. Exit wound at surface on corresponding level. Scar 5" x 1.5" (surgical), puckered and adherent. All movements of elbow, hand, wrist and hand normal. Grip good, no wasting of muscles. Recommend pension gratuity of 5%.*

Jayne clicked forward a few pages. The pension amounted to fifteen pounds, three shillings and sixpence.

Jayne sighed 'The man got shot and hospitalised for two months and all he gets is fifteen pounds,' she said out loud.

As she spoke, her father's head moved for the first time. Jayne held her breath.

His head rested slightly to the left, but he continued to sleep deeply.

She breathed out.

She mustn't speak loudly any more, it obviously disturbed him. It was strange how even in the deepest, drug-fuelled sleep people were still aware of ambient noise.

She returned to her laptop. The second document was the strangest. In 1921, Tom re-enlisted in the army. This document contained a full description of the man at that time.

*Apparent Age: 34 years and 4 months.*
*(To be determined given the instructions given in the regulations for Army Medical Services)*
*Height: 5 feet 8 inches*
*Weight: 140lbs*

*Chest: 37 (when fully expanded)*
*Range: 2 inches (chest expansion not large)*
*Complexion: Sallow*
*Eyes: Grey*
*Hair: Light*
*Religion: Roman Catholic*

She could imagine him standing in front of the medical examiner. A careworn man, not terribly fit or healthy. Why had he rejoined the army?

The final document was his discharge papers, processed 178 days later. This time the document was short and blunt.

*Discharged as medically unfit. Was unable to perform duties as a soldier due to lack of strength in his arms.*

So they refused to pay him for his injury but were quite willing to criticise him for not being able to carry his kit. The world hasn't changed much since then, Jayne thought.

Her eyes wavered out of focus and she pinched the top of her nose. God, she was tired.

Tomorrow morning, she would meet up with David even though it was Christmas Eve, and take him through all the documents. At least he would be able to know more about his great-grandfather and his life as a soldier in the First World War. She messaged him to arrange the meeting.

For now, though, she would just take a little nap. She glanced across at the father, his face at perfect rest.

She closed her eyes.

Her mobile phone rattled in her bag.

*No, I'm not answering it.*

Then it began to ring, each call tone rising in volume. She snatched it out of her bag, checked her father quickly and ran out into the corridor.

'Yes?' she snapped into the speaker.

'Hi there, Mrs Sinclair, it's Herbert.

## Chapter Nineteen

Friday, December 25, 1914 – Christmas Day
No-man's-land, Wulverghem, Belgium

Tom Wright stared at the German's outstretched arm for a few seconds, wiped his own against his woollen overcoat and shook the man's hand. 'Were you the sniper two nights ago?'

'Should keep your head down, Tommy.'

'And so should you.'

'I suppose I'll have to, especially with blokes like you around. Want a cigarette?' The man opened the box to reveal an elegant row of thin white tubes, laid one on top of the other.

'Don't mind if I do,' said Tom, reaching into the box and lighting the cigarette. 'Where did you learn to speak English?' he said, releasing a long draught of smoke into the misty air.

'Manchester. I was a mechanic in Chorlton-on-Medlock. Had an English girlfriend, Rose West. You want to see her picture?'

He reached deep into his grey overcoat, pulling out a battered leather wallet and opening it to reveal a picture of a young woman, taken in a studio on Oxford Road.

'She's a bonny lass, right enough.'

The German stared at the picture for a moment before placing it carefully back in his wallet. 'Haven't heard from her since the war started.'

They looked behind them. Men had come out of the trenches on both sides and were standing along the edge of the parapet.

'We have a truce for today, Tommy, yes? What you say?'

'It's Tom, not Tommy.' He glanced back at the British line behind him again. 'I dunno, my officer, he...'

'My captain, he wants to bury our dead.'

Tom Wright checked the British lines again. Captain Lawson was advancing towards him with Bert in tow.

'Looks like he's coming anyway, Fritz.'

Over his shoulder, he could see a very tall German officer in a grey overcoat with a fur collar coming from their lines.

'It's Harald. Harald Kanz. Not Fritz.'

'Okay, Harald.'

The two officers met in the middle of no-man's-land, saluted each other and stood at attention for a moment before reaching forward and shaking each other's hands.

'Captain Peter Lawson, 6th Battalion, the Cheshires.'

'Graf Alfred von Kutzow, Captain, 35th Landsturm Regiment.'

They both stood back for a moment before Captain Lawson began speaking again. 'Damn good weather. Best we've had all week.'

The German officer looked up at the sky. 'Should hold for the next couple of days. Maybe a touch of snow tomorrow.'

'You speak very good English for—'

The officer smiled. 'For a German? I went up to Oxford in '10. Balliol.'

'I was at Manchester. Chemistry.'

Again, an awkward silence between the two of them. This time it was the German officer who spoke first. 'Look here, we can't have our chaps killing each other on Christmas Day. It isn't cricket. Let's call a truce and bury our dead.'

'Just for today?'

The German pulled his sleeve back to reveal an expensive Swiss watch. 'Until four p.m., what say you?'

'Your artillery won't shell us?'

'They would prefer to be eating their Christmas dinner, I think.'

Captain Lawson stared at the British wire, with the dead German body stretched across it. 'Till four it is. But no approaching our lines. We stay here in no-man's-land.'

'Agreed.'

The German officer turned and waved to the troops standing above their parapet, bringing them forward.

Slowly, step by step, they moved through their wire, stumbling through the former turnip field that was no-man's-land.

Captain Lawson turned to wave the Cheshires forward, but found they were already leaving their trenches in droves.

Both sides met in the middle. At first, the greetings were awkward; only a few of the Germans spoke English and none of the Cheshires spoke German. But through a combination of sign language and gestures, they all began to communicate.

Around Tom and Harald, the men were all talking at the same time. Even Bert was chatting away to a German corporal, who was nodding his head.

'It's a good day, Tom.'

'It is, Harald. If you don't mind me asking, why are you fighting for Germany? You were living in Manchester...'

'Same reason as you. I was called up and went back to fight for my country. Why are you here?'

Tom Wright shrugged his shoulders. 'I wanted to fight for the King.'

'And I fight for the Kaiser.' He smiled ruefully. You know, we should be fighting the French, not each other. What did you do, Tom?'

'In Stalybridge?'

Harald nodded.

Next to him, Harry was hugging a German soldier, swapping his soft forage cap for a much warmer balaclava. Another German was carrying a box of cigars, handing them out to the British soldiers, who eyed the brown tubes suspiciously.

'What do I do with this, sir?' one of them asked Captain Lawson.

'Smoke it, Rawlinson. Not a bad make.'

A German wearing a camouflaged Picklhaube reached forward and a flame shot from his lighter. Rawlinson leant forward and lit his cigar, inhaling deeply before collapsing in a bout of coughing.

'Got a bit of bite, this one. Not a bad smoke, though,' he said, large puffs of smoke leaving his mouth and frosting in the cold air.

Tom Wright turned back to face Harald. 'I was a button maker. Silk buttons, for gentlemen's waistcoats.' He noticed the silver buttons on Harald's tunic. 'I'd love to have one of those.'

'Swap you for one of yours?'

Harald produced a pen-knife and began to cut the cotton attaching the button to his tunic. 'See, it's my regiment's crest and number around the edge.'

He handed it and the pen-knife over to Tom, who cut one of the Cheshire buttons off his tunic. He'd find another from somewhere. 'The crest is a star with the regiment's name inside, and within that, a cluster of oak leaves with a single acorn. Just brass, though. None of the silver stuff for us squaddies.'

'My button isn't silver either. Silver gilt. None of the real stuff for us.'

Around them, all the soldiers were swapping their hats, coats, buttons, trench tools, tobacco, sausage, toffee, tins of bully beef, tins of blackcurrant jam and scarves.

Captain Lawson was smoking a cigar with the German officer, both men looking as relaxed as if they were at their respective clubs, chatting about the latest test scores from Lords.

On the right, a queue of German soldiers was kneeling down to have their hair cut by Captain Lawson's batman, whose profession had been a hairdresser in civvy street. His scissors moved with the speed of a scythe through their long curly locks, leaving clumps of brown, blond and black hair at his feet.

Tom watched as men rubbed their newly shaven heads and smiled gap-toothed for cameras which had appeared suddenly from both sides. A German was marshalling a group of men into a wedding photo of soldiers, each man's arm around the other like a bride and groom. Bert was pictured next to an enormous German who towered over him.

'David and Goliath,' Captain Lawson said.

'Samson and Delilah,' answered the German officer.

Harry was bartering some army boots he had found in a dugout for a bottle of schnapps, but the German seemed reluctant to part with his alcohol.

'Listen, I'll throw in my hat. Now you can't say fairer than that, can you?'

The German shook his head and walked away, still with his bottle of schnapps grasped tightly in his hand.

Another group of men, a mixture of Germans and British, were placing the bodies of the men who had fallen during the fighting one week ago on to stretchers and carrying them off to the left, where the remains of a wooden barn still stood between the two lines. One of the British sergeants was digging shallow graves through the frosted soil for the bodies, the spade making a rasping noise as it cut through the hardened soil.

One by one, the bodies were carefully laid to rest beside each other, after removing all identification and personal effects. A German came running back from his lines with two pieces of wood, which were quickly nailed together to make a makeshift cross.

There were seven bodies in all, both German and British. Tom and Harald strolled over to join the battalion's priest as he said a short service of commemoration for the dead men. Around twenty men from both sides were assembled around the graves. All removed their hats and bowed their heads in prayer.

'God, our Father. On this, Your special day, remember these men who gave their lives so that we may live. Your power brings us to birth, Your providence guides our lives, and by Your command we return to dust.' He paused for a moment, as if gathering his thoughts. 'Lord, those who die still live in Your presence, their lives change but do not end. I pray in hope for their families, their relatives and friends, and for all the dead known to You alone. In company with Christ, who died and now lives, may they rejoice in Your kingdom, where all our tears are wiped away. I ask also that You remember those still living today, the men from both sides, gathered here to commemorate their comrades. May You protect and guide them today and evermore.'

Tom and Harald both crossed themselves and placed their hats back on their heads.

'I hope to go back to Manchester when the war is over,' said Harald. 'I still have my bike there, a Royal Enfield. Fast as a cheetah and twice as elegant.'

'Made like a gun and goes like a bullet,' said Tom.

'You know the slogan?'

'And the bike. It's got a 45-degree V-twin, with an inlet-over-exhaust valve.'

'And the glass oiling system.'

'With kickstart. No more pedalling like a maniac to get it going.'

Harald stepped back and appraised Tom. 'You know your bikes.'

'Will she still be there when you go back?'

Harald shrugged his shoulders. 'Perhaps, perhaps not. But the war can't last much longer. We will go home soon. The English cannot keep fighting.'

'Sounds like you have learnt nothing about us, Harald. We always keep going, against the odds. It's part of our character.'

'But don't you want the war to end?'

'Of course. I want to be back with Norah, and Hetty, and John and Alice.' Simply speaking their names made him pause for a second and catch his breath. 'But we won't give up and go home with our tail between our legs.'

'And neither will we.'

They walked on a few more steps in silence. Around them, the other soldiers were swapping cigarettes; Turkish for Virginia, German cigarettes for those given in Princess Mary's Christmas box. A cloud of smoke hung over their hands as each tried the other's tobacco.

'Perhaps the Kaiser and your King George will sit down one day and thrash it all out over the dinner table. They are cousins, after all.'

Tom tried to imagine it happening, but couldn't see it. There was too much bitterness on both sides.

Harry came running towards him, rushing back towards their lines.

'Where you going?'

'I got an idea, be right back.'

Two minutes later he returned, with a gigantic smile beaming across his face and a football under his right arm.

## Chapter Twenty

Friday, December 25, 1914 – Christmas Day
No-man's-land, Wulverghem, Belgium

'Right, you lot, who's for a game of footie? Germans against Cheshires.'

Harry dropped the ball on to the ground then flicked it up with his boot, bouncing it twice on his knee before booting it towards a crowd of men who were standing around smoking and chatting.

A German controlled it with his chest and tapped it back to Harry.

'Not bad, son, where on earth did you learn to do that?'

'I played for VfB Leipzig in this year's Viktoria Meisterschaftstrophäe. We were beaten by those Bavarian bastards, Furth.'

'Bad luck, I hate getting beat too. Was that your championship or your cup?'

'Both. We have regional leagues and then there is a final where all the winners play each other.'

'Sounds complicated.'

The German shrugged his shoulders. 'It's Germany.'

'Fancy a kickabout?'

'I'll put my coat down for a goal. You do the same over there, beside the wire. Willi, give me your coat.'

The soldier ran to place his coat down on the ground, measuring eight paces from the other. He then rolled up the sleeves of his thin grey shirt and tucked the ends of his trousers into his socks.

'That one looks professional. You playing, Bert?'

'Me? No chance, I prefer to puff on my pipe and stand and watch.'

'Lazy sod. Come on, Tom, put your coat and scarf down.'

Tom ran to help Harry measure out the goalposts, laying the coats on the ground just in front of the wire.

'I'll be goalie, Harry. Can't run very much any more.'

'What's the prize, Tommy?' the man from Leipzig shouted as he assembled his players.

Harry shrugged his shoulders.

The German captain held up a bottle he was about to trade with Captain Lawson. 'Schnapps for the winning team.'

'Whisky from our side,' added Lawson, holding up a bottle of Dreadnought Scotch above his head, showing it to all the men.

Suddenly, more of them from both sides were taking off their coats.

'And the winning team keeps the ball,' shouted Harald.

'Aye, that's fair. Winners keep the ball,' agreed Harry.

He booted the ball down towards the Germans, gathered fifty yards away. One of them immediately began to dribble it back towards the British goal over the hard ridges of the former turnip field.

'Tackle the bugger,' shouted Harry.

A sergeant from C Company came rushing out of nowhere, still wearing his sheepskin jacket and smoking a cigarette, to take the ball off the tricky German winger and kick it towards their goal.

The player from Leipzig controlled it in one go and floated over a perfect cross for his friend to rise in front of Tom and nod the ball over the line.

'One-nil to us, Tommy.'

Tom ran back to retrieve the ball from the German wire. He noticed a hand sticking out of the frozen ground like it was a plant emerging in spring. The nails were yellow, with dirt encrusted beneath them. The sleeve was just visible above the ground. The man, or the corpse as it now was, could have been German, English or French.

'Hurry up, Tom, we've got to equalise.'

He bent down to pick up the ball, trying not to look at the hand.

But he did.

That was a man once. A man like him; breathing, loving, with a family somewhere who would never know where his life ended.

'Hurry up, Tom. War'll be over by the time you get back.'

Tom picked up the ball, snagging the leather on the barbs of the wire.

He booted it down towards Harry and ran back to his place between the goals.

More men had joined in now. There seemed to be about twenty per side. The ball bobbled and wobbled on the hard ground as it hit men's knees and boots and bodies.

The match flowed from end to end. There was no real organisation, no real positions; each man chasing after the brown leather ball, kicking it as hard and as far as he could in any direction, as long as it was away from him.

Harry seemed to be the captain.

'Over here, over here.'

'Nah, not like that, at me feet. I like it at me feet.'

'Tackle him, Ron, don't let him past.'

The Cheshires scored twice and then the Saxons equalised. The light was beginning to weaken as the sun sank lower and lower in the sky.

The ball was bobbling through, a German in mad pursuit. One on one, versus Tom. The man looked up, hesitating for a second. Tom saw his chance, rushing out to dive at his feet, snaffling the ball just as the man was about to shoot.

'Well played, that man,' shouted Captain Lawson.

Tom kicked the ball towards the German line, and it struck two heads before landing at the feet of a fat miner from Poynton who booted it goalwards.

'You know, I missed the end of the cricket season. Who won the championship?' said Captain von Kutzow.

'It was Surrey this year, with Middlesex second. My team, Lancashire, were very poor. The weather, you know.'

'Yes, Manchester is famous for its sunshine.'

Captain Lawson glanced across at his German counterpart, who was casually smoking his cigar, blowing the smoke out into the air above his head.

'Hammer it, Ron!' It was Harry shouting.

The ball had broken free from a morass of players to Ron Harris, their youngest soldier. Officially he was eighteen, but everybody knew he was just sixteen, having joined up the day war was declared.

Ron tapped the ball with his right foot, took careful aim and shot just wide of the right-hand post masquerading as an army overcoat.

'How could you miss that?' Harry shouted.

The German goalie booted the ball downfield. Harry rose to nod it forward but it slid off the back of his head to Harald, who was standing just in front of the goal. The ball bobbled on a ridge of frozen mud, hit his knee and slowly dribbled over the line past a diving Tom.

All the Germans jumped up in the air and surrounded an ecstatic Harald.

The sun was going down behind the British lines and the bright light of thirty minutes ago was already being replaced by the soft eerie glow of a winter twilight.

Captain Lawson looked at this watch. 'We should be going back now. Four p.m.'

'I suppose we should,' the German officer said regretfully, sucking on the stub of his cigar.

Captain Lawson blew two long blasts on the whistle attached to a lanyard, imitating as competently as he could the sound of a referee calling time.

All the players stopped and looked at him.

'Time's up. Match is over.'

'But it can't be, they're leading three-two,' said Harry.

Captain Lawson's tone changed. 'The game is over, Larkin.'

Harry kicked the ground in front of him. Tom took the chance to shout, 'Three cheers for the Saxons. Hip hip, hooray. Hip hip, hooray. Hip hip, hooray.'

This was answered by the Germans in a more robust fashion.

The German officer shook Captain Lawson's hand. 'It was a pleasure meeting you.'

'And you too.'

'Perhaps, after the war, if Surrey are playing Lancashire, we could enjoy watching the game together.'

'I'd love you to be my guest at Old Trafford. Jack Sharp versus Jack Hobbs would be a sight to see.' Captain Lawson reached into his breast pocket. 'I always carry this with me, don't know why really.'

He handed over a small red book with gold lettering on the front.

'A Lancashire membership card? I'll keep it safe till the war ends. We'll meet again in the member's bar at Old Trafford.'

They shook hands once more and both set off briskly for their respective trenches without looking back.

The rest of the men were gradually drifting to their lines. Bert had said goodbye to his newfound friends and was now clutching a German sausage under his arm. Harry was picking up his overcoat from close to the wire, still shaking his head and kicking the ground.

Tom had already wrapped his scarf around his neck and fastened the collar of his greatcoat tight against the cold of the night.

Harald strolled over, carrying the ball under his arm.

'You won this game fair and square.' Tom held out his hand.

'I was lucky. First goal I ever scored.'

'It won the game. You can keep the ball.'

Harald stared down at it for a moment, before handing it with both hands back to Tom. 'No, you keep it. No winners today, just friends playing football.'

Tom thrust it away back to Harald. 'Keep it. Give it back to me after the war, when you come to Manchester for your bike.'

Harald smiled, tucking the mud-covered ball under his arm. 'But you must promise me something if you can.'

'Of course.'

He ran over to one of the Christmas trees standing near the German lines, scrabbling amongst the pine needles for a moment before running back to Tom, avoiding the pointed barbs of the wire.

'You must give me your address, so I can return it.' He held out a label. Tom could see green lettering on one side. The other was clear. He took out his pencil and wrote his name, service number and address on the label.

Harald searched in one of his inside pockets, finally producing a large fountain pen. He unscrewed the top and wrote '3-2' in large letters on the back of the label, next to Tom's name and address.

'A memory of our game and of the result.'

Harry ran over. 'Better get back to our lines, Tom. We're the last lot.'

Tom stared out across no-man's-land. It was empty of soldiers now, just the three of them standing out starkly against the wire and dark earth. The place was still and quiet, the air hardly moving, as if held in place by the ghosts of the men who had spent the afternoon there.

Tom shook Harald's hand. 'See you in Manchester after the war.'

Harald smiled. 'Not if I see you first, Tom.' Then his face changed. 'I wrote this letter for Rose. Could you post it for me? It will be easier on your side.'

Tom took the letter, looking down at the address.

*Rose West,*
*26 Makin Street,*
*Chorlton-on-Medlock,*
*Manchester.*

'We'd better hurry, Tom.'

Above their heads, the first Very shell had exploded in the sky; a bright flash slowly drifting down to earth.

'Bye, Harald, look after yourself.'

'Bye, Tom.'

They waved to each other one last time as they headed back towards their lines.

Above their heads another Very light arced into the sky.

## Chapter Twenty-One

Friday, December 25, 1914 – Christmas Day
No-man's-land, Wulverghem, Belgium

That night, Tom, Harry and Bert sat in their usual positions, crouched over a brazier. It was a cold, frosty evening with the moon casting eerie shadows over no-man's-land.

For once, their sector was quiet. The distant lightning of an artillery barrage was absent. The faint crump of the trench mortars was silent. The crack of the sniper's rifle could not be heard.

The Very lights still illuminated the sky, but that was out of habit rather than anything else.

'Not a bad bunch of lads,' said Harry.

'Who?'

'Fritz. Just like us, really.'

Bert sat up straight. His pale green eyes could just be seen, glinting in the firelight, sandwiched between the peak of his cap and the edge of a green scarf wrapped around his face and ears. When he spoke the sound was muffled. 'Don't be thinking like that. Those thoughts get you killed.'

'I was just sayin'—'

'Don't "just say" anything. Given a chance, he'll kill you tomorrow soon as look at you. That's his job and why he's here.'

'Nah, he won't. Not the player from Leipzig. We is mates. He wouldn't shoot me.'

Bert pulled the scarf away from his mouth. 'Mates, my arse. If his hofficer tells him to shoot you, he's gonna do it. Same as if Captain Lawson gives you the order.'

It was the most animated Tom had ever seen his friend. 'Take it easy, Bert, Harry was just—'

'Harry was just getting his stupid self killed. Today was good, but tomorrow and the next day and the day after that, we are going to be killing them and they are going to kill us. Get it straight in your head.'

Harry laughed. 'With a bit of luck we'll be pulled out of the front line and back into billets tomorrow. Then nobody will be killing anybody.'

Bert's hand snaked out and clamped Harry's throat. 'If I tell you to kill, you kill. Understand?'

Harry nodded, his eyes wide with fear.

Bert released his grip and stared into the fire. 'Had a friend in the Boer War; thought like you, he did. One day, he was lighting a cigarette for a prisoner, turned his back and the man knifed him. I shot the man dead on the spot but it was too late, George was dying.' He shifted his eyes from the fire to Harry. 'You know what he said before he died?'

Harry shook his head.

'"Forgive him, Bert, forgive him." Well, I never did. A soldier's job is to kill or be killed. That's why I'm here. That's why you're here. That's why Tom's here. Get it?'

Bert went back to staring into the embers of the brazier, his bottom lip covering his moustache as he clamped his jaw shut.

It was Tom who spoke first. 'We're not machines, Bert, and neither are they. It's Christmas, a time of love and understanding.'

Bert snorted.

'I watched you out there today. You were having as much enjoyment as the rest of us.'

'I saw you too,' said Harry, 'filling your pipe with that German tobacco like you were stuffing a turkey.'

Bert's jaw relaxed. 'Was good tobacco.'

He reached into the voluminous pockets of his greatcoat and pulled out a pipe, its porcelain bowl decorated with the crest of the 35th Regiment. 'One of the buggers gave me this, filled it with tobacco too.' He took a spill from the brazier and touched it to the bowl of the pipe. After a few seconds, a cloud of smoke issued from his mouth, filtering through the walrus moustache. 'Draws well, a lovely smoke.'

'Here's what I think, Bert,' said Tom. 'And, as it's Christmas, think of it as my gift. This war's not going to last for ever, the killing's not going to carry on. But one thing it's taught me is if we can't learn how to get on – the Germans and the French and the Brits and Uncle Tom Cobbley and all – well, if we can't learn to get on, there ain't much hope for us or our children.'

'Is that it?'

Tom nodded.

Bert puffed on his pipe. 'Well, happen you're right, Tom Wright, happen you're right.'

## Chapter Twenty-Two

Saturday, December 23, 2017
Macclesfield General Hospital, Cheshire

Jayne went back into her father's ward. He was still lying there, asleep on the bed, his back supported by three pillows. The machines still beeped quietly beside him.

The covers on his bed rose and fell slowly with each inhalation. He looked peaceful now, the most comfortable she had seen him in a long time.

Was he ready to die? She had read somewhere of people giving up on life, simply deciding they didn't want to go on with the struggle any more.

But she knew her father, he never gave up on anything. There was his new wife, Vera, and his travels with her. And, of course, there was Jayne. They still had so much to share, so much to say to each other.

The machines beeped endlessly on. Strange how one's life was measured by the metallic pings of a heart monitor. A sharp angular green line of life. Was it true that when we are born, our hearts had just so many beats assigned to them and, once they were used up, our lives were finished? She was sure it was just an old wives' tale, one of those propagated by her mother.

Her father was a fighter; he would never give up.

She sat down on the hard chair next to his bed. A nurse had drawn the curtains to stop the night lights coming in and disturbing the other patients. Like her father, they were sleeping too. Were they all under sedation, or was sleep the body's way of healing itself?

She would ask the doctor when she saw him next time. Meanwhile, she had the puzzle of Tom Wright to solve.

She picked up her laptop, thought for a moment and then googled 'Christmas 1914'.

A host of images and Wikipedia entries popped up within 0.12 seconds. They were a bit slow today. She clicked on Google Images and saw a black-and-white picture of a group of soldiers, both German and English, stood smoking in no-man's-land. Two British officers, one wearing a macintosh and the other smoking a pipe, mingled with both sides. It was as if they had been asked by the photographer to line up and smile for the camera.

Another shot was a close-up of four Germans and one British soldier. Nobody was smiling at the camera; they all looked bedraggled and careworn. The eyes of one of the German soldiers were drooping and tired, a look that said 'I don't want to be here, in this war'.

She clicked the next photograph, of three German officers smiling at the camera this time. Behind them an English officer was chatting away while, next to him, an old English sergeant leant on a long stick, calmly puffing on a pipe.

The war seemed a world away as they fraternised, all wrapped up in a variety of scarves, balaclavas, caps, overcoats, macs, sheepskins, woollen mittens and heavy mud-caked boots.

Most seemed to be smoking or exchanging stories, posing for the camera with a self-consciousness which was not seen so often in the age of the selfie.

There were also pictures of football games; men in puttees and khaki against Germans in field-grey and long boots. But on clicking the links, Jayne found that most of these pictures were re-enactments or re-imaginations. There seemed to be no pictures of football games taken on Christmas Day 1914.

She scrolled down further and clicked on the front page of the *Daily Mirror*, dated January 8, 1915 – a full two weeks after Christmas. The headline read **'An Historic Group. British and German Soldiers Photographed Together.'** Below was a picture of a line of British and German soldiers in front of the bare branches of a dead tree sticking out of the ground. The men were huddled together, as if encouraging the photographer to hurry up because it was cold.

Beneath the picture a caption read: **'Foes become friends on Christmas Day, when British and Germans arranged an unofficial truce. The men left the trenches to exchange cigars and cigarettes and were even photographed together. This is the historic picture and shows the soldiers from opposing Armies standing side by side.'**

Jayne scanned the rest of the page. Just so his readership wouldn't forget there was a war on, the editor had placed two other large pictures below. One was of a smashed German artillery piece with the headline, **'German Gun Shattered By British Shells'**. Next to it was a picture of a man and dog, captioned: **'Dog Saves Sailor's Life'**.

'Mustn't forget the human interest stories even in the middle of a war,' she muttered out loud.

Her father snuffled in his sleep. Was the oxygen mask too tight? He seemed to be breathing well and the mask covered his mouth and nose without digging into the skin. She decided to leave it. The nurses knew what they were doing, and she was sure Vera had checked before she had left.

She went back to her chair and itemised what she had found out.

Tom Wright had apparently taken part in one of the most famous episodes in the First World War; the Christmas Truce. He probably exchanged the button with a member of a German Regiment during the ceasefire on Christmas Day, along with the label from one of the Christmas trees the Germans had put up in front of their trenches.

Some reports had the men playing games of football with the Germans. Is that what the numbers '3-2' on the label showed?

Was this the result of a game they played that day? And if it was, was the football used to play the game? Could the old leather found by David Wright be the very football they had used?

Jayne recognised all the conditional words she was using. Apparently. Probably. Could.

She laughed to herself. That was the problem with genealogical research; you could guess at what happened from the facts, but you could never be absolutely certain.

And then she remembered the opening line from her presentation. 'The past is a foreign country. They do things differently there.'

She yawned, checking her watch: 9 p.m. Vera would be here soon for the night shift. Her father was sleeping quietly now; already his colour had gone from a pale white to a healthier rosy hue.

Perhaps he was getting better.

It was time to rest for an hour. She made herself as comfortable as she could on the hard chair, folded her arms and closed her eyes.

She would finish her research tomorrow morning and then meet David afterwards.

In the meantime, what she needed above all was sleep.

As her eyes closed, in that still moment between consciousness and sleep, a thought flitted across her mind.

*How can I prove this was the ball?*

## Chapter Twenty-Three

Saturday, December 26, 1914 – Boxing Day
No-man's-land, Wulverghem, Belgium

As Harry had predicted, the company was moved out of the front line on Boxing Day, pulling back east of Bailleul on December 28 for much-needed rest and recuperation.

They packed up their gear, and handed over their brazier and orange crates to the relieving soldiers of the Bedford Regiment.

'What's the line like?' asked a sergeant.

'Quiet.'

The sergeant peered over the parapet.

'I wouldn't do that, though. Their sniper's good, have your head off.'

The sergeant ducked down as if he had already been hit. 'Thanks for telling me. Your wire looks clean, no bodies hanging off it. Last trench I was in stank to high heaven. Had to cover our mouths all the time.'

'We buried them.'

'Germans too?'

'All of them,' Bert said, 'by the tree stump on the left.'

'Heard you lot had a bit of a party on Christmas Day.'

The three friends glanced at each other but didn't say anything.

'Anyway, that's all over. My lieutenant has ordered a raiding party for this evening. We're to snatch some of their men. This live-and-let-live stuff has to stop.'

'Don't get killed,' said Bert quietly, hefting his kit bag on his back. 'Don't want to have to bury you when we come back next week.'

With that, they stumbled down the trench, walking their weary way through the support trenches and the rear lines to their new billets.

At one point, Tom thought he could hear firing from the section of the trench they had just left.

'Sounds like war has started again, Bert.'

'Reckon you're right, Tom.'

Off to the left was the soft *crump* of mortar shells as they were fired into the German line.

Harry picked up a newspaper lying in the mud, dated November 9. He scanned the sports headlines. 'Looks like United lost, hammered by bloody Everton. Oldham still top of the table, beating Bradford. Wednesday lost at Spurs. At least the football is still going strong.'

Tom thought of his family and his wife. How was their Christmas? Did the children enjoy themselves? How did Norah manage to cope on her own?

He would have to write and tell her what had happened to him in the middle of no-man's-land. How did he make friends with the enemy?

And then the image of Harald, ball tucked under his arm, strolling jauntily through the wire back to the German trenches and whistling 'Oh Tannenbaum' came back to him.

He whispered a simple prayer beneath his breath, hoping both he and Harald survived this war.

For their friendship.

## Chapter Twenty-Four

Sunday, December 24, 2017 – Christmas Eve
Cheetham Hill, Manchester

Jayne met David and his son outside the antique-cum-bric-a-brac-cum-militaria store in the north of Manchester.

She knocked on the front door and it was immediately answered by the spotty-faced youth called Gerald.

'I hope Herbert's not done a runner.'

The grey hair and stubbled chin of the antique dealer looked over his assistant's head.

'You know, you have a disappointing opinion of my character and human nature in general, Mrs Sinclair.'

She brushed past him to enter the shop. It was still as dirty as ever. 'Years of experience dealing with people such as yourself, Herbert.'

'I've been going straight for five years,' he said indignantly.

'Just means you haven't been caught for five years.' Before he could answer, she asked, 'Do you have any coffee in this godforsaken hole, preferably served in a clean cup?'

He looked down his nose at her. 'Follow me through to the back room.'

All of them danced between the furniture, weaving their way to a curtain behind the till.

Herbert pulled it open with a flourish to reveal a small, clean and well-stocked dining room and kitchen, with a microwave oven, convection oven and a brand new coffee machine standing on a counter.

'I am impressed, Herbert. You surprise me.'

'I like a nice cup of coffee in the morning, Mrs Sinclair. What would you like?'

He held open a box filled to the brim with Nespresso capsules.

'I hope these didn't fall off the back of a lorry.'

'Actually, I bought them in the Trafford Centre, if you must know. A friend works there.'

Jayne frowned, but chose a golden capsule.

'Dulsão. One of my favourites too.' Herbert chose a strong Kazaar for David and an Indriya for himself.

'Before we start on the coffee, where are the football, label and button, Herbert?'

The antique dealer opened a suitcase sitting on the counter. Inside were two cloth bags and a plastic folder. He handed the folder to Jayne.

Through the clear plastic, she could see the green printing and recognised it now as a stylised Christmas tree with the words *Weihnachtenfest Baum* at one side.

'Thank you, Herbert.'

'I thought it best to protect it, given it's so valuable.'

'How much is it worth?' asked David tentatively.

Herbert shrugged. 'Whatever people will pay for it. These are extremely rare. I was offered six hundred quid for it last night.'

'You told me four hundred,' said Jayne.

'He upped his offer this morning, Mrs Sinclair. But I reckon if we put it in an auction, the sky's the limit.'

'But we're not selling, are we, Martin?' David said forcefully.

Herbert raised his eyes to the ceiling and then reached for a small cloth bag. 'I took the trouble of giving this a light polish. I hope you like it.' He handed over the silver button, now gleaming against a maroon velvet cloth.

The raised letters for the 35th Regiment were cleaned of all blemishes. Before they could thank him, he opened the other cloth bag, producing a small but beautifully formed leather ball.

'It only needed a bit of tender loving care. Still a few cracks in the leather, but with the gentle touch of Herbert's hands it was soon looking great.'

'I did it,' piped up a voice from behind them. Gerald had his hand up.

'My assistant helped. Under my guidance, of course.'

'It's beautiful,' said Martin. 'It looks like a real football.'

'Thank you for all your help,' said his father.

'Think of it as my Christmas present for your son.'

Jayne shook her head. 'Herbert, you never cease to surprise me.'

The old man looked embarrassed, mumbling, 'I'll make the coffee.'

As the wonderful aroma of coffee filled the kitchen, Jayne explained what she had discovered, with Herbert's help.

'So it seems your great-grandfather, David, took part in one of the most famous events in the First World War – the Christmas Truce. I downloaded the Cheshire Regiment's war diaries from the National Archives this morning. Both the first and the sixth battalions were in the trenches opposite the Germans on Christmas Day as part of the Fifth Division. I also checked in a couple of histories of the period. Apparently, the 6th Battalion played a game of football against the 35th Regiment.'

Martin held up the ball.

'So this football was the one they used.'

Jayne shook her head. 'It could have been the one they used, but without documentary evidence we will never know.'

Martin's face fell.

His father put his arm around his shoulders. 'Don't worry, at least we know your ancestor fought in the war and was a hero in the trenches.'

Martin frowned. 'But it would have been nice for Chris to know that this ball was used then. Somebody actually played a game of football with it. Cheer him up in the hospital.'

'I may be able to help.'

Jayne turned to Herbert Levy, who was standing next to the Nespresso machine. 'This is a morning of surprises.'

'You don't know, do you?'

'Know what?' Jayne asked.

Herbert twisted his head. 'So this is what it feels like to be you, Mrs Sinclair, always knowing something that other people don't.' He stood taller. 'Hmm, I like this feeling, a sense of superiority...'

'What is it, Herbert?'

'I checked last night. There is a Military Museum in Chester, which holds all the archives for the Cheshire Regiment. I called them this morning and as it's Christmas Eve, they are only open until three p.m. today.'

'Good, maybe you can pay them a visit one day with Martin and Chris,' said Jayne.

Herbert held his hand up imperiously. 'I haven't finished yet. I talked one of their volunteer researchers and they have a war diary written in 1914 by an officer of the 6th Battalion. A Captain Lawson, apparently. It mentions the football game, but they wouldn't tell me any more.'

Jayne checked her watch. She was due back at the hospital at three p.m. to relieve Vera.

She made a quick decision, putting her coffee down on the bench. 'Come on, David and Martin.'

'Where are we going?'

'Where else? Chester. It's only an hour away.'

## Chapter Twenty-Five

Sunday, December 24, 2017 – Christmas Eve
Cheshire Military Museum, Chester

The museum was a sandstone Georgian building in the middle of Chester, surrounded by the walls of the medieval castle.

'Is the castle real?' asked Martin, staring up at the battlements.

'Of course,' answered Jayne. 'Chester has been around for at least two thousand years. It was one of the major cities of Roman Britain and was then called Deva. Ever since, it's been occupied.'

'Romans? We studied them at school. Hadrian's Wall and all that.'

They parked up outside the museum next to a statue of Queen Victoria and opposite the Crown Court.

A tall, straight-backed man with white hair and a military bearing was waiting for them in the hall, wearing a maroon polo shirt with the museum's logo prominently displayed.

'Jayne Sinclair?' He stuck out his hand. 'I'm Reg Atkinson, volunteer researcher. I'm here to help you today. I believe you're interested in World War One?'

'Actually, a specific part of World War One. The Christmas Truce.'

Reg Atkinson smiled. 'Mister Levy said you were interested in that period. May I ask why?'

135

'My great-grandfather was there,' said Martin. 'Tom Wright was his name. Or, at least, we think he was there. We found these things in a box in the attic.' He held up the bag with the label, the football and the button.

'Do you have anything in the archives that could help us?' asked Jayne.

'Do you know which battalion he served in?'

'The 6th, we think.'

'Well, they were in the front line at Christmas in 1914.'

'We know, the war diaries told us as much.'

The volunteer researcher looked directly at Jayne. 'And may I ask your interest in this man?'

'I'm a genealogical researcher, looking into Tom Wright for his great-grandson.'

David stuck out his hand and Martin waved.

'That's wonderful. We don't hold any records for soldiers here, but we do have some individual diaries for 1914, written by the officers of the regiment. They are far more descriptive and personal than the official records. I remember one in particular has an entry on the Christmas Truce. Would you like to see it?'

Jayne nodded. 'It sounds perfect.'

'We have to complete the form and I'm afraid there is a donation of twenty pounds for research. It all goes to help the museum.'

'That's no problem.' Jayne reached for her wallet but was stopped by David.

'I'll pay, Mrs Sinclair, you've done enough.'

With the forms completed and the research fee paid, they walked through the museum, past models dressed in the various uniforms of the regiment thorough the ages, to the World War One exhibition area.

Inside was a lifelike mock-up of a trench, complete with periscope, entrenching tools, sandbags, dugouts and vicious-looking barbed wire.

'The Cheshire Regiment served in all the major battle grounds of the First World War, with over eight thousand men giving their lives. Virtually every town and village in the county suffered casualties. If you come this way, I'll take you through the archive section.'

They were shown into a small book-lined room with three large desks in the centre.

'If you wait here, I'll get the diary. Sorry, but you'll need to wear gloves when handling it.' He pointed to a pile of freshly laundered cotton gloves. 'It was given to us by Captain Lawson's widow in his memory.'

Jayne thought for a moment. 'Before you go, Mr Atkinson, you might want to see the objects left by Martin's great-grandfather, Tom Wright.'

'I'd love to.'

Martin opened the bag while Reg Atkinson put on a pair of gloves. The young boy pulled out the box with the button first. The old man examined it carefully. 'Seems to be a uniform button of the 35th Landsturm Regiment. Definitely First World War. Interesting.'

Martin passed across the plastic folder with the label.

'Also looks like First World War vintage. A label for something. I'm afraid my German is pretty spotty.'

'According to our sources, it's a Christmas-tree label from 1914.'

The eyes of the old man narrowed. 'I see where you're going with this.'

Next, Martin pulled out the football from its cotton bag.

The researcher's eyes widened. 'It's not what I think it is...is it?'

Jayne shrugged her shoulders. 'We don't know, that's why we're here. These footballs were given out to soldiers by the *Daily Mirror* in 1914.'

'The 6th Battalion played football with the Germans in no-man's-land during the truce...'

'Now you know why we need to check your archives. Was this the ball they used?'

Reg Atkinson's hand moved to his mouth. 'I'll be right back.'

## Chapter Twenty-Six

Sunday, December 24, 2017 – Christmas Eve
Cheshire Military Museum, Chester.

Reg Atkinson was true to his word, returning five minutes later accompanied by another volunteer researcher.

'This is Henry, he'll be helping me.'

Henry rubbed his hands. 'It's the most exciting Christmas we've ever had.'

Reg was carrying two box files in his gloved hands. 'Before we look at the diary of Captain Lawson, you said that your great-grandfather's name was Tom Wright, didn't you?'

Martin nodded.

'Do you remember his regimental number?'

Without any prompting, Martin recited it by heart. .A quick knowing glance from Reg to Henry. 'We thought so.' He opened one of the box files. 'These are original copies of the Cheshire Regiment's magazine, the *Cheshire Oak*.' He placed an old yellowing paper magazine on the table. 'If you'll turn to page twelve of the March 1918 edition.'

David opened it. On page twelve was a slightly blurred picture of a young man in uniform shaking hands with a nurse.

The caption read: **'Private Thomas Wright 12725 says goodbye to one of the "angels" before returning to the Regiment in France.'**

'That's…my…great-grandfather?'

'I remembered seeing it when I catalogued the magazines.'

David continued staring at it. 'He looks so young and fit here. I only vaguely remember him as an old man.'

'We'll look at Captain Lawson's diary now. Unfortunately it only goes up to March thirteenth, 1915. He was killed in action on the fifteenth.'

Reg opened up the second box file and brought out a small orange diary, dated '1914' in gold on the cover. Inside was one page for each day of the year.

'He was a regular officer and marched off to war with the 6th Battalion when it was sent to France in November. As you can see, he was pretty diligent about keeping the entries.'

Finally, he opened the pages headed in neat handwriting 'Christmas Eve, 1914'.

Jayne began to read out loud.

*Christmas Eve, 1914.*

*Well, that's another day over. Casualties were light, just one man shot this morning as he ran back to the support trench. He died of his wounds before the medics could get to him, but at least they removed his body. The rest of the day was quiet. We heard artillery but that seemed to be coming from the West. Thank heavens it was nowhere near us.*

*As dusk was falling, the most amazing events took place. Along the German lines, Christmas trees started to appear on the parapets of their trenches. Of course, I called the men to arms and thought about ordering a volley to be fired in their direction but decided to get orders from Divisional HQ. They told me the same thing was happening up and down the line and not to fire unless Fritz fired first.*

*I ran back to our trench and the Germans were singing carols. It was the strangest sound I'd ever heard! The lovely* melody of *Silent Night* hovering over no-man's-land. Just yesterday they were firing at us and today they are singing carols. No one will ever understand the workings of the teutonic mind.

Our lads joined in, with Quartermaster Sergeant Davies being an excellent leader of the Cheshire's front-line choir.

If I live to see the end of this war, I don't think I will ever experience a stranger day than today.'

She paused for a moment. 'Can you imagine singing carols with the Germans? What an amazing time it must have been.'

She turned the page and began reading the next entry.

*December 28, 1914.*

*I'm writing this from the billets in Bailleul. Three days ago, we passed Christmas Day in the trenches. The morning was foggy so I sent some men back to Stinking Farm just behind our line to see if they could catch a few of the wild chickens that scratched the ground there. Private Harris was particularly good at diving on them from a great height. We managed to catch only five scrawny birds but they were better than nothing for Christmas.*

*While we were away, one of our men, Private Wright, went out into no-man's-land to parley with a German. I arrived back to see them both chatting away nonchalantly, smoking a cigar as if it was the most normal thing to do on earth.*

*I went out with Sergeant Simpkins and we were met by one of their officers, Von Kutzow, a Magdalen man. After agreeing on a truce until four p.m., the men spent the rest of the day mixing with the Germans. They were slightly older than us — a reserve regiment, though, like the Sixth. I managed to exchange a belt buckle, some cigars, schnapps, some tea tablets and twenty Turkish cigarettes for my old penknife and a bottle of whisky. I think I got the better part of the deal.*

*After we had buried the dead and eaten the chickens, Private Larkin produced a football from somewhere and the men began to play. The game was pretty chaotic - a kick and rush affair rather than something properly organised. But I'm afraid we were beaten by the 35th Regiment, even though Private Wright had a particularly fine game in goal. The Germans took the ball as a trophy for winning the game. At four p.m., we all shook hands and returned to our trenches.*

*Divisional HQ were not happy and we received a stern rebuke from above, commanding that it was never to happen again. The football game we arranged for New Year's Day has been cancelled.*

*Merry Christmas.*

'So we know they played football; a sort of kick-about game like we would play in a park. And he mentions that Private Wright organised the truce and played in goal.'

'Could that be my great-grandfather?'

'Quite possibly, although there may have been other men with the surname Wright in his company. All it says was the Germans won the game, and as a prize, they were given the football.'

Martin picked up the plastic folder, which held the German label. 'I wonder... Could the numbers "3-2" be the score for the match? Did the Germans win three-two?'

Jayne stared at the label. 'Possible. It makes sense. It also explains why it's written in different handwriting. A German must have written it.'

'So if the Germans were given the ball, this can't be the one they played with?' said David.

Again, another glance between the two research volunteers.

'We think we have the answer,' said Reg. 'Look in the box.'

## Chapter Twenty-Seven

Monday, December 24, 1923 – Christmas Eve
22 Elgin Street, Stalybridge

They waited quietly for him. Norah was fussing in the kitchen, checking the goose in the oven. Hetty was helping her with the vegetables. John was reading a book, as he always did, whilst Alice was doing her needlework beneath the old lamp, unperturbed by the tension in the house.

Tom was standing alone in the front parlour, leaning on the fire surround and smoking his pipe, the fingers of his left hand tapping irritably on the seam of his trousers. The clock on the mantelpiece next to his head ticked on loudly.

He had received the letter a week ago and responded immediately:

*I would be happy to meet again. Perhaps you would care to come to our humble home for supper on Christmas Eve? Later we could go to Midnight Mass if you are not feeling exhausted by your travels.*

He wondered how Harald had obtained his address. Then he remembered writing it on the Christmas-tree label. Harald must have kept that old paper all these years.

Tom glanced at the clock. *Was that the right time?* He had pawned his watch the week before to ensure the children had something for Christmas. One day he would get it back, when he found work again.

The year had been difficult. His arm had been giving him gyp for a long time and the army had finally released him, saying he was medically unfit to be a soldier. He had been fit enough to charge across no-man's-land against the Siegfried Line in 1918, but now the war was over, the army didn't want him any more.

Bastards.

The dole was a pittance, barely enough to feed a mouse. 'A home fit for heroes'? More like a country fit for tramps. At the election two weeks ago, he had voted for Labour and Ramsay MacDonald for the first time. Change was needed, the quicker the better.

He walked over to the curtains and checked outside. The streets were already dark and the lighterman hadn't arrived yet to light the gas lamps. He hoped the visitor could find their home on his own.

As well as the watch, they had sold a few pieces of furniture from upstairs to make sure they had one good Christmas. Tom had his pride, what man didn't? He was going to make sure his family, and his visitor, had a decent Christmas Eve.

And besides, he had a job interview at the Post Office next week. Good job, a postman. Letters were always going to be sent. His arm may be kiboshed but his legs were as strong as ever.

The squeal of brakes outside the house. Norah ran into the parlour, followed by Hetty. He crossed back to the curtains and peered through them.

A dark figure, looking large in his thick woollen overcoat, was getting out of an enormous car, stopping to help a woman descend. The door of the car was being held open by a chauffeur dressed in a grey uniform.

'That's a Rolls-Royce, that is. Seen pictures of them.' John was beside him, peeping round the edge of the curtain.

A sharp rap on the door.

Tom froze.

It was Norah who spoke. 'Shouldn't we open it?'

He stood still for a moment, before clamping his pipe between his teeth, hoisting up his braces and marching out of the parlour to the front door.

Through the small window he could see a shape distorted by the glass.

Another rap on the door, this time louder.

Tom took a deep breath and opened it.

Harald Kanz stood on the doorstep.

'My old friend Tom, it is so good to see you again.'

Before Tom could react, the man had folded him in his arms, hugged into the embrace of the warm overcoat.

He held him tight for twenty seconds before stepping back. 'You haven't changed, but you see I have put on a few pounds since our last meeting.' He patted his large stomach.

Harald still had his accent; that strange mix of Manchester English and German that Tom remembered so well.

'Where are my manners? Please, let me introduce my wife, Rose.'

She held out her hand. 'I received the letter from Harald you sent all those years ago, Mr Wright. As you can see, we managed to stay in touch despite the war.'

'I was the happiest man in the world when Rose agreed to become my wife three years ago.'

'Tom, whatever are you doing? Please invite Mr Kanz into our home,' Norah called from the parlour door.

'Call me Harald, please, *gnädige Frau*.'

'And I'm Rose,' added his wife.

Tom stepped aside. 'Please come in. It's not much but it's our home.'

'You do me a great honour, inviting me.' Harald stepped across the threshold, greeting the children lined up beside the door of the front parlour. 'And who are these beautiful children?'

'This is Hetty, my eldest; John, who is twelve; and Alice, the youngest.'

Harald shook each of the children's hands in turn before he was shown into the parlour. 'A lovely family room, Tom.'

He headed straight for the picture of the family above the mantelpiece, staring at it for a long time before saying, 'And a beautiful family. You are a lucky man.'

'Would you like something to eat?' said Norah. 'It's not much but it's what we have for Christmas. Goose, carrots, roast potatoes and gravy.'

'And there's Christmas pudding and custard for afters. I made it six weeks ago,' said Hetty. 'With Mother's help, of course,' she added, her face reddening.

'That sound wonderful. And to help it down, I have brought some wine, beer and schnapps from Germany.'

There was a knock on the parlour door. John opened it to find the chauffeur standing in the entrance, carrying parcels and bottles.

'Let us eat your wife's wonderful supper first, then we will open our presents. Yes?' said Harald.

The chauffeur placed his gifts carefully in the corner and left.

Tom looked around the crowded parlour. The arrival of Harald had been like a whirlwind in the house. A pleasant whirlwind. bringing with him all the joy of Christmas.

Norah came in with the goose and all the trimmings and laid them on the parlour table. 'Please, help yourself, Rose.'

'It looks wonderful. A proper Christmas feast.'

They all tucked in to the food, the children waiting respectfully, if hungrily, for the guests and their parents to eat first. Tom carved the goose, of course, ensuring Harald and Rose received the best bits of the breast and the thigh.

Afterwards, both guests were stretched out on the sofa.

Harald patted his stomach. 'What a wonderful supper. That is the best meal and food I have eaten all year.'

'Some more Christmas pudding, Rose?'

She smiled and puffed out her cheeks. 'I couldn't eat another morsel.'

'Another glass of wine, Harald? Takes me back to France, does drinking wine.'

Tom topped up both their glasses. Neither Norah nor Rose were drinking.

'And now it is time to open the presents, yes?' Harald hauled himself off the couch and limped over to the gifts stacked in the corner, selecting one after reading the label. 'This is for young Alice.' He handed over the gift.

'What do you say, Alice?'

'Thank you, Mr Kanz.' She stood there, holding it in her arms.

'Don't be shy. Please open it.'

The young girl carefully undid the gold ribbon and the wrapping paper. Inside was a straw basket filled to the brim with different coloured cottons, needles, frames and wools, all perfect for needlework and crochet.

'How did you know?' gasped Norah.

Harald touched his nose. 'I have my secret knowledge, yes? And now for John.'

The boy didn't wait, but stood in front of Harald with his arms out.

'My little bird tell me you like cars, John, is that true?'

The boy nodded.

'Here is my favourite car for you.'

John ripped open the present to reveal a model of a Rolls-Royce Silver Ghost Tourer.

The boy's eyes lit up. 'It's great, thank you, Mr Kanz.'

'This was given to me by Sir Henry Royce himself.'

The boy took his new car out into the corridor.

'And now we have Hetty, and Tom's beautiful wife, Norah.' He passed across two presents.

'I picked out these two silk shawls myself from Afflecks. We can always change them if they are not to your taste.'

'Oh no,' said Norah, staring at her shawl, 'it's beautiful.' Hetty had already run off to look at hers in the hall mirror, tripping over John, who was racing his car.

'What's this, Father?' Alice was holding up a crisp new five-pound note.

'I took the liberty of adding a little something for each child. I hope you don't mind, Tom. It's for their education.'

'I couldn't possibly accept, Harald, the ch—'

'Tom,' Harald interrupted, 'I will only waste the money and children should receive a proper education, don't you think?'

'Yes, but...'

'Good, that's settled,' said Rose. 'Can I help you with the washing up, Norah?'

'I couldn't possibly...'

'I spent half my life as a housemaid. It's the one thing I do well.' She tilted her head to indicate they should leave the parlour.

Norah understood immediately. 'Children, go to your rooms and play with your gifts.'

'But, Mother!'

'Up you go.'

In a minute the men were alone in the parlour, sipping their schnapps and staring into the red embers of the fire.

'You've been too kind, Harald,' Tom finally said.

'No, it was you who was kind that night before Christmas.'

Tom smiled. 'You would have done the same.'

'I still remember that day out in no-man's-land. Perhaps the best day of my war.'

'The best day of anybody's war.'

'I was badly wounded the following year at Ypres. My officer, Captain von Kutzow, was killed in the same action.' He took a swallow of schnapps. 'Myself and Rose can't have children, but she married me anyway.'

'Sorry to hear it, Harald.'

A moment's silence between them.

'But we enjoy our life. And, in many ways, being invalided out of the army was the best thing that ever happened to me. I opened a garage in Dresden and now have over a hundred workers. We also have the licence to sell Rolls-Royces in Germany. Mister Benz is not happy. It's why I am visiting Manchester and Crewe. What about you, Tom?'

Tom shrugged his shoulders. 'Wounded twice, but managed to get through somehow. It's not been easy, Harald, but we survived. Despite everything, we survived.'

He swirled the clear liquid around his glass. On the mantelpiece, the clock ticked remorselessly on.

'Remember Harry?' Tom eventually said.

'The footballer?'

'Lost his left leg on the Somme, they amputated it. He never recovered, took to drink. I heard he killed himself two years ago.' Tom was silent for a moment.

'And Bert,' he continued. 'He died with Captain Lawson in March 1915. Funny thing is, Bert was carrying his officer's body back to our lines when he was hit. Beneath all the show and bluster he was a brave man, a true soldier.'

'Too many good men died.'

Tom raised his glass. 'To the soldiers.'

Harald raised his glass to and drank, finishing his schnapps. 'And I didn't forget you, Tom, I have a present for you too.' He handed over the last parcel.

Tom put his glass down and took the square parcel, staring at it in his hands.

'Please open it, Tom.'

Slowly, carefully, Tom removed the ribbon and the wrapping, pulling out a leather football with a Christmas-tree label attached to the lacing.

There, in that small front parlour, with its ticking clock and dying fire, Tom finally started to sob for all those who would never return and the innocence of the Christmas Truce that was lost for ever.

His friend, once his enemy, put his arm around his shoulders and held him close.

On the mantelpiece, the clock ticked on.

## Chapter Twenty-Eight

Sunday, December 24, 2017 – Christmas Eve
Cheshire Military Museum, Chester

Jayne peered into the file. Inside was a letter addressed to the curator and postmarked April 4, 1967.

'Apparently, this was sent to us not long after Mrs Lawson donated her husband's diary,' said Reg.

Jayne pulled out a single sheet of paper from the envelope. The handwriting was weak and fragile, the letters of each sentence shaky and cramped on the page. She began to read out loud.

*Dear Sir,*

*Further to the donation of my husband's diaries to the museum, I am reminded of a quite peculiar occurrence that happened in the days before Christmas 1923.*

*I received a visit from a small, rotund man with a peculiar accent - a mixture of Manchester slang spoken with a pronounced German twang. His name, as I remember it, was Harald Kanz. A strange fellow he was too.*

*He sat in my living room and talked of my husband. Well, you can imagine my surprise at a German saying he knew my husband. I have never forgiven them for his death, and the death of my brother at Passchendaele in 1917. My first instincts were to ask him to leave, but he was a persistent fellow and gradually told me his story.*

*He was one of the German soldiers who took part in the Christmas Truce that my husband mentions in his diary. I'm*

151

sure you have read the page. Apparently, my husband and his officer, a Captain von Kutzow, became friends on that day. His officer died in April 1915, not long after the truce. He told me his officer's dying words were to return something to my husband. The something turned out to be my husband's Lancashire County Cricket membership card.

I don't know if you are aware, but my husband and I both loved cricket. Many a happy day was spent in the Ladies' stand at Old Trafford, watching them play. I haven't been back there since the end of the war, it brings back too many sad memories.

Harold Kanz said he was also going to visit another friend he had met that day. Private Tom Wright. I must admit that all this talk of friendship between the opposite sides unnerved me. But I suppose a strange bond existed between the men in those early days of the war.

He told me he wanted to return some personal effects to the man. I found out that these effects were a football and a Christmas-tree label. They seemed inconsequential to me, but the man said they were as important to him as the membership card was to my husband.

For the next fifteen years, I would receive a Christmas card every year from him, always arriving on December 23. After 1938, though, the Christmas cards stopped. I don't know whether it was because he had died or he had suffered under Mr Hitler's regime. Whichever it was, I never heard from him again.

I have enclosed the membership card in the envelope. I don't think it is interesting enough to go on display, but I find the story of how it was returned to my family fascinating.

Thank you for your kind words on my donation to the Cheshire Military Museum. My husband loved the Regiment and I see it as only fitting that his wartime effects should find a home there.

I remain, etc,
Joy Lawson

Jayne upended the envelope. From it fell a small square red book, about two inches by two inches. Printed on the cover in gold letters was 'Lancashire County Cricket Club Member 1914'.

She opened it. Inside were the usual rules and regulations for membership, plus a fixture list for the 1914 season. The back page had a light brown stain. Blood, perhaps.

'So it was one of the Germans who returned the football and the label, that's how my great-grandfather had them,' shouted David.

'And they remained carefully stored away in a box in the attic until you found them a week ago,' said Jayne

'Wait till I tell Chris, he'll be so happy.'

'It can be your present to him tomorrow on Christmas Day,' said David.

'Right, Dad, brilliant.'

Reg coughed. 'What are you going to do with the objects? You know they are quite valuable, not mentioning the importance they have as historical artefacts.'

Jayne glanced across to David.

The man scratched his head. 'I don't know. We've only just found out what they are.'

'Let's talk to Chris tomorrow, Dad. Let him decide.'

## Chapter Twenty-Nine

Monday, December 25, 2017 – Christmas Day
Christies Hospital, Manchester

Chris was already sitting up in bed waiting for them. Around him the ward had been decorated with all the trimmings of Christmas; red glitter balls, a silver Christmas tree, dashing Santas with laden sleighs, two elves naughtily playing, and a rainbow of streamers on the ceiling, accompanied by balloons and shining stars.

The young man's chemo had been postponed until after Christmas so he could enjoy the holiday with his family and friends before he went into isolation.

'Merry Christmas, Chris,' his father shouted from the door, carrying the presents on to the ward.

Martin rushed in to to hug his brother. 'Chris, we've been investigating, like real detectives. Tom Wright fought in the war.'

'Which one?'

'The First World War. He was wounded twice.'

'Calm down, Martin, don't get Chris too excited,' cautioned his father. 'Let's give him the Christmas presents first.'

'Is it about the things we found in the attic? Are they valuable?' asked Chris.

'They are, but the value is more in what they tell us about one of your ancestors.' Jayne sat on the end of the bed.

'Chris, this is Jayne Sinclair, she's the genealogist who's been performing all the research for us.'

Chris's eyes lit up. 'Wow. You've found out all about the silver button?'

'We think so. Of course, we can't be absolutely certain, the events were over a hundred years ago, but we're pretty sure what happened. I'll tell you all about it after you open your presents.'

'Great.'

'Your aunt Dora got you these.' David passed across a pair of socks that looked like Birkenstock sandals.

'She always gives me socks.'

'And I'm sure you'll send her a card to say thank you, won't you?'

Chris smiled. 'Of course, Dad. What did you get me?'

'Two things, hope you like them.'

Chris ripped open the boxes. Inside one was a retro arcade-game machine, already loaded with twenty old games.

'Brilliant.'

'It'll help you pass the time. Open the other present.'

Chris ripped the wrapping paper off. Inside was a personalised Manchester United history book.

'It's got all the teams and the players since 1888,' said David

'The nurses told me Sir Alex may be coming round later today. I'll get him to sign it.'

'And you should get him to sign this too.' David brought out another present from behind his back.

'The new kit with Pogba's on the back! Thanks, Dad.' He leant forward to give his father a hug.

'I think I've got you the best present,' said Martin. He produced an unwrapped box from the Tesco bag.

On the cover it said Poo Head! The Poo-flinging Game!.

'You put on this cap, I fling the poo and you have to catch it on your head.'

Chris and Martin immediately began flinging plastic poo at each other.

'Boys, enough. It's Christmas, play nicely,' said David ineffectively.

'My Christmas present to you isn't something you can hold, but it's a story that happened one hundred years ago,' said Jayne.

Both boys stopped flinging the plastic poo.

'In 1914, a brave man called Tom Wright went off to war, leaving behind his wife and three children: Hetty, John and baby Alice. He had been a piecer before the war, working in a big mill in Stalybridge.'

'What's a piecer?'

'It's a man who crawls under the cotton-spinning machines and pieces together the broken threads.'

'Sounds dangerous,' said Chris.

'It was,' replied Jayne. 'Many people were injured by the fast-moving parts of the machine. Anyway, this man, Tom Wright, went off to war...'

Jayne then told the story as she had managed to piece it together, bringing in all the different threads: the German button, the label, the old football and, above all, the relationship that had existed between two men who became friends despite the war.

'So you see, we think this German soldier, Harald Kanz, returned these things to your dad's great-grand-father after the war, probably when he visited Man-chester in 1923.'

Chris held the old football close to his chest. 'So this football was used for a game in 1914?'

'We can't be absolutely certain, but all the evid-ence points that way.'

'Why were these things hidden in the attic?'

Jayne shrugged her shoulders. 'We'll never know. Perhaps the memories were too painful for Tom Wright. Or perhaps he just wanted to forget about that period of his life. You know, many of those old soldiers never spoke about the war. They never told anybody what they endured.'

'It sounds sad,' said Chris.

'It is and it isn't. We believe my great-grandfather took part in one of the most amazing events of the whole war. In December 1914, on Christmas Day, all across the front line, men from both sides put away their weapons for a few hours and just talked to each other,' said David.

'That's why these things from that time. The button, the label and the ball are so valuable. They are a little piece of history, Chris.'

Chris hugged the ball tighter to his chest.

Jayne continued speaking. 'Your family has to decide what to do with them now. There are three options. You could keep them, you could sell them, or—'

'We could give them to the museum you visited. Then everybody could see them and read my ancestor's story,' said Chris.

'Is that what you both want to do?' asked David.

The boys nodded their heads.

'Then it's decided. We donate them to the museum. Reg and Henry will be extremely happy, I think.

Chris frowned. 'But one thing I don't understand. If Tom Wright fought in the war, he would have medals, right? What happened to them?'

Jayne and David looked at each other. It was a question they should have asked. 'We don't know, Chris. I guess we'll never know.'

She stood up. 'It's time for me to go now.'

157

'Before you do, Jayne, I have one more Christmas present for Chris. I spoke to the oncologist earlier. After the lumbar puncture, they tested your white blood cells and the leukaemia hasn't spread to the central nervous system – and it's chronic rather than acute. He seems to be positive that the chemo has a good chance of working.'

'That's great news, Chris. Your best Christmas present ever,' said Jayne.

Chris nodded. 'It is, but this comes a close second,' he said, hugging the football to his chest once more.

## Chapter Thirty

Monday, December 25, 2017 – Christmas Day
Macclesfield General Hospital, Cheshire

After leaving Christies, Jayne drove down the A523 to Macclesfield. The roads were empty. On Christmas morning, most families were spending time together, swapping presents, eating chocolate and nuts, preparing turkey or simply enjoying the special joy that is Christmas morning.

Jayne was driving along the empty road, reliving memories of Robert and their life together.

The time they had gone to Blackpool and she had so wanted to ride the Big Dipper but her mother had said no, until Robert stepped forward to accompany her even though he was scared of heights. As she had hollered and whooped, he'd spent the whole ride with his eyes closed and his hand tightly gripping hers.

Or the time she had come home from school with her uniform ripped and torn after a fight with a boy who had tried to bully her. Robert had taken her out to buy a new uniform before her mother saw the damage to the old one.

Or the time when they had sat and listened to Candle in the Wind over and over again on the day of Princess Diana's funeral, both of them with tears in their eyes while her mother looked on in bemusement.

She realised she had shared so many wonderful times with Robert. A man who was more of a parent to her than her mother had ever been.

She parked the car and hurried up to his ward. Vera was waiting beside his bed, her book open and her knitting in the bag by her side.

Robert was still sleeping in his bed, but the oxygen mask was no longer covering his mouth.

'How is he?' she whispered.

'Fine. I think he's improving. The doctor said he didn't need oxygen any more. And look, colour has returned to his cheeks and his hand isn't so clammy.'

Jayne heaved a sigh of relief. If Vera thought he was getting better, it was a good sign.

'How are you?' she whispered again.

'Not bad, a little tired but I can manage.'

'Why are you two whispering?' The voice was weak and crackly. 'I can hear everything, you know.'

Jayne and her stepmother looked at each other. It was Vera who spoke first.

'How long have you been awake?'

'Quite a while. Time for me to get up.' He tried to lift his shoulders from the bed.

Vera was up in a flash, pressing his body gently back down on to the bed. 'You stay right where you are, Robert Cartwright,' she ordered. 'You're not going anywhere.'

His eyes were open now and Jayne was stunned by the brightness of the blue irises.

'You gave us a scare, Robert.'

'I know. Sorry, lass. What day is it?'

'Christmas Day.'

'I could murder a turkey leg.'

'I'll see what the hospital has to eat. You must be starving.' Vera rushed out to the nurses' station.

'I've been so worried, Robert.'

'I can imagine, lass.'

'Vera has been brilliant, staying here with you.'

'She's one in a million, lass. I'm so lucky to have found her.'

Jayne glanced towards the door.

'I hope you realise why I've been nagging you so much to look into your own past, Jayne. I'm not going to be here much longer.'

'Shhh, Dad, don't talk like that.'

But she knew what he said was true. He wasn't going to be around much longer. But whether it was two days or ten years, she vowed to enjoy every second or every minute with him.

'You know he was my best friend.'

'Who?'

'Your real father. He wasn't a happy man and he wore his heart on his sleeve...'

'Shhh, Dad,' Jayne interrupted. 'Save your strength, we'll talk about it later.'

'No, we'll talk about it now,' Robert said forcefully. 'You see, I think he's still alive.'

THE END

# Historical Note.

The events of December 1914, later called the 'Christmas Truce', have been well documented. In this novel I have attempted to bring a more personal exploration of the experience and its aftermath.

My own interest in the time began with a visit to the National Football Museum in 2015, which commemorated the period and displayed a football and a diary from Lt Charles Brockbank of the 6th Battalion, the Cheshire Regiment.

I spent a long time researching the Christmas Truce. There are some excellent histories available from David Boyle's *Peace on Earth*, John Hendrix's *Shooting Stars*, Malcolm Brown and Shirley Seaton's *Christmas Truce*, Stanley Weintraub's *Silent Night* and many others.

In addition, I looked at the newspapers of the time. The story seemed to break quickly in a letter sent to the *London Evening News*. This was quickly followed up by *The Times*, the *Daily Mirror*, the *Daily Sketch* and other newspapers. Even local journals got involved; letters from soldiers were published in the *Nottingham Evening Post*, the *Gloucester Journal*, the *Aberdeen Journal* and, in Cheshire, by the *Macclesfield Times*, describing the Christmas Truce. These letters were sent to loved ones and forwarded on to the newspapers.

But the truce wasn't an organised event. Most of the commanding officers – certainly on the British side – hated fraternisation with the enemy. The commander of the British Second Corps, General Sir Horace Lockwood Smith-Dorrien, believed this proximity posed 'the greatest danger' to the morale of soldiers and told Divisional Commanders to explicitly prohibit any 'friendly intercourse with the enemy'. In a memo issued on December 5, 1914, he warned that 'troops in trenches in close proximity to the enemy slide very easily, if permitted to do so, into a "live and let live" theory of life'.

There had been attempts to organise a formal truce, notably by Pope Benedict XV, but these were firmly rebuffed by the governments of both sides.

But nonetheless, a truce happened between the opposing forces on Christmas Day 1914. Why?

From reading the reports of the time, it seems to have been a spontaneous eruption of good will. It must be remembered that in many cases, the front lines were often less than two hundred yards apart and, in one case, the gap between the two trenches was less than fifty yards. Both sides were used to shouting across to each other, usually insults or slanders on the other's manhood. In addition, the dreadful attrition of the later years, with its mass slaughter at Verdun, the Somme and Passchendaele not yet having taken place. The soldiers facing each other were often professionals, or at least had spent some time in the reserves.

The truce didn't happen everywhere. Indeed, both sides suffered casualties on Christmas Day in certain parts of the front. And it does seem to have been confined to the British and German troops. There are few reports of fraternisation between the French and the Germans.

The events basically happened as I have described in the book. The troops sang carols to each other on Christmas Eve. They met and congregated in no-man's-land on Christmas Day, swapping food items and bits of kit, burying their dead and then returning to their respective lines as the sun went down.

For the next few days, little fighting or firing took place. Indeed, the 'live and let live' policy seemed to have been instituted by the company commanders of both sides.

However, such a peace did not continue. By New Year, most troops had been rostered out of the front line, with fresh troops introduced. By New Year, the High Command had regained control, issuing dire threats to the men and their officers, preventing any further fraternisation.

There has been one note of controversy in the historical accounts: Did the football games actually take place?

The popular myth is of an organised game with rules, referees and sides. However, the truth as described in letters and diaries of the period seems to be much less formal. The men simply found a ball, laid hats and coats down as goals, and then proceeded to play informally, with often a hundred men on each side. The sort of kick-around in the park we all played as youngsters.

The 6th Battalion of the Cheshire Regiment did indeed play a game of football with the 35th Landsturm Regiment, as described by Lt Brockbank in his war diary. However, he did not record any score and it was played with a small rubber ball rather than any of the Mitres donated to the troops by the Daily Mirror.

I have dramatised the events slightly in the interests of the novel.

Although the war was to last three more Christmases, the events of 1914 were never repeated on any large scale. The Christmas Truce was a one-off event, a coming together of men to reach the hand of friendship across no-man's-land.

As ever with the Jayne Sinclair Genealogical Mystery series, I have kept as closely as possible to the actual events. I have used the 6th Battalion of the Cheshire Regiment as my lead soldiers. The men of this battalion were all reservists, many of whom were mill workers in the cotton towns surrounding Manchester: Glossop, Stalybridge, Hyde and Stockport.

The experience of the early days of war was as I have described, but I have brought in some details from other areas of the front lines to add detail. The work by John Hartley, The Sixth Battalion in the Great War, was extremely useful for the movements and biographies of the men involved. I am also indebted to the volunteers of the Cheshire Military Museum in Chester for their wonderful information. The museum – and the city – are well worth a visit for all those interested in English history from Roman times.

In all, over 8000 men from the Cheshire Regiment died in World War One – a loss that can still be seen in the numerous war memorials across the mill towns of the area.

One last set of records I consulted were the official War Diaries of the Battalion in the National Archives. These are daily records of the activities, casualties and movement of the men under their commanding officer.

Funnily enough, there is no mention of the fraternisation on Christmas Day in those records. As always, the first casualty of any war is truth.

I'll leave the last word on the Christmas Truce to Arthur Anderson, the last surviving soldier who took part, speaking in 2003 when he was 108 years old:

*I remember the silence, the eerie sound of silence. Only the guards were on duty. We all went outside the farm buildings and stood listening. And, of course, thinking of people back home. All I'd heard for two months in the trenches was the hissing, cracking and whining of bullets in flight, machine-gun fire and distant German voices. But there was a dead silence that morning, right across the land as far as you could see. We shouted 'Merry Christmas', even though nobody felt merry. The silence ended early in the afternoon and the killing started again.*

In a time of war, he found peace.

If you enjoyed reading this Jayne Sinclair genealogical mystery, please consider leaving a short review on Amazon. It will help other readers know how much you enjoyed the book.

## Other books in the Jayne Sinclair Series

### The Irish Inheritance

When an adopted American businessman dying with cancer asks her to investigate his background, it opens up a world of intrigue and forgotten secrets for Jayne Sinclair, genealogical investigator.

She only has two clues: a book and an old photograph. Can she find out the truth before he dies?

### The Somme Legacy

Who is the real heir to the Lappiter millions? This is the problem facing genealogical investigator, Jayne Sinclair.

Her quest leads to a secret buried in the trenches of World War One for over 100 years. And a race against time to discover the truth of the Somme Legacy.

### The American Candidate

Jayne Sinclair, genealogical investigator, is tasked to research the family history of a potential candidate for the Presidency of the United States of America. A man whose grandfather had emigrated to the country seventy years before.

When the politician who commissioned the genealogical research is shot dead in front of her, Jayne is forced to flee for her life. Why was he killed? And who is trying to stop the details of the American Candidate's family past from being revealed?

In her most dangerous case yet, Jayne Sinclair is caught in a deadly race against time to discover the truth, armed only with her own wits and ability to uncover secrets hidden in the past.


### The Vanished Child

What would you do if you discovered you had a brother you never knew existed?

On her deathbed, Freda Duckworth confesses to giving birth to an illegitimate child in 1944 and placing him in a children's home. Seven years later she returned but he had vanished. What happened to the child? Why did he disappear? Where did he go?

Jayne Sinclair, genealogical investigator, is faced with lies, secrets and one of the most shameful episodes in recent history as she attempts to uncover the truth.

Can she find the vanished child?

The book is the fourth in the Jayne Sinclair Genealogical Mystery series but can be read as a stand alone novel.

Every childhood lasts a lifetime.

.